I0620237

EIGHT MONTHS IN CYRANDOR

By Auburn Sommer

Published by

Say Press
P.O. Box 691063
Orlando, FL 32869-1063

ISBN 978-0-9914793-3-7

Dedicated to my parents and siblings, who created wonder in my youth, to savor as an adult.

CHAPTER ONE

Grandpa said that Uncle Cheech would be taking care of me. He was a pleasant enough sort of man, I suppose. Plump and always smelled of cigarettes. I didn't know that's what he smelled like. To me he just smelled like Uncle Cheech. He was a little mysterious. Not the kind of Uncle you knew how to get along with right away. Nor the sort who knew quite what to do with children. Let alone me. My fingers were often black with dirt, and since I had a habit of wiping hair out of my face, it was inevitably marred with dirt as well. My view of the world was often parted in multiple places by a strand or two of dark brown hair. I doubt Uncle Cheech knew what to do with that, either.

Don't misunderstand me, though. He wanted to take care of me. He loved my folks. I guess he just understood them better. I guess I did too. Uncle Cheech and I didn't quite understand each other, though. And it started with his very name. Cheech. His real name was Calvin. I still don't know how it became Cheech. But there it was. And he lived in this town called Cyrandor. I'd never visited that place before, but it sounded like some kind of mythical city. It must have hidden secrets and fantastical adventures. Or perhaps it was just a town. I suspected the latter but hoped for something better. Cyrandor. For eight months.

Grandpa never said why, though. He just said.

***

His house seemed like a quiet little cottage. If it were in a painting, you might have seen puffs of smoke billowing from the chimney. But I never did. Not at first. It was a little bit less inviting than that. And there didn't seem to be much of a town at all. Not that I could see. But I was only just settling in.

He fixed me a lovely dinner that night I arrived. He smiled a lot, but he was missing one or two teeth up front. His face was unshaven, and a little prickly when he kissed me goodnight as he tucked me in. He tried awful hard that night to assure me of my welcome. He even said that eight months will come and go before I know it. And that he and I - we'd get along just fine. I believed him. But I wondered still, why Cyrandor?

No child would have slept well on such a night. It was a new place. New sounds. New shadows. I'd rather not recall too much of it. Just understand that I grew accustomed to the sounds and shadows, just as I had my own home's sounds and shadows. But there was a strong comforting aroma at Uncle Cheech's house. In fact, it smelled just like Uncle Cheech. But only at night after I went to bed.

***

I woke nearly nine times that night. The final time, I sat up and surveyed the little corner room where I was staying. The bed was nothing much. A simple cot with four blankets. I was plenty warm for the night but shivered with nerves and anticipation for most of my rest.

Beside the cot was a wooden trunk sitting on its side. It doubled as a nightstand that way. There was a candle and matchbook resting dimly on its surface. I had no need to light it however as the lanterns that Uncle was using flooded their light around the corner.

There was a stack of story books on the wooden floor near the foot of the bed. No doubt acquired for my stay. I had no intention of reading quite yet this morning. I simply sat still and waited for the light of dawn. The windows could not hide its arrival.

As I lay down again, I remembered what Grandpa told me before I left for Cyrandor.

"Rosa, life will bring you many questions. You may not always find the answers. But sometimes, the answer is in the journey itself."

I wasn't sure what he meant by that. I really wasn't sure about too many things. But Grandpa also said that it would take an awful big dog to weigh a ton. I kind of figured that much was true. And as my eyes closed once more in dreams, that dog came into focus.

***

That time, I slept well past breakfast. It wasn't intentional. But I suppose I needed the rest. Uncle Cheech wasn't too pleased though. Or at least, I assumed he wasn't. When I awoke, I found a cold plate of scrambled eggs and no sign of Uncle. I ate the eggs.

My nightgown and bare feet were reminders of the mystery of my temporary home. I wasn't used to the wooden boards, nor the draftiness in the morning. There were too many trees to block the sun's warmth through the windows. Mother and Father's house was considerably warmer this time of year. I glanced at the empty fireplace but instead took a seat near the stove.

I couldn't imagine where Uncle had gone. I didn't even know what he was. Was he a laborer? A doctor? Certainly not a doctor. Perhaps a lumberjack? Maybe Uncle Cheech hadn't any job at all. Maybe he was still close by.

I stepped out onto the porch of the old cottage. It wasn't a very large porch. It wasn't a very large cottage. And it was just as I suspected - no rocking chairs. But no Cheech either. I sat down anyway. A very puzzled look appeared on my face, I'm sure, but I masked it quickly. Uncle or no Uncle, I wanted to know about Cyrandor.

***

The view from the porch was pleasant. The yard was mostly dirt with a few patches of grass here and there, and some fallen twigs and branches from the many trees that inhabited the property. But that was not too unlike home. Perhaps, there were fewer trees back home. I spied a low branch where I imagined I might be spending some afternoons pondering the wonders I had discovered during my stay.

Uncle Cheech's house was the only one I could see. The dirt lane ran to hide in both directions. I was determined to find something – anything – that would add intrigue to my visit. If it wasn't in one direction, it'd be in the other. I skipped down the steps of the porch, picked up a medium sized stick and headed to the right.

I took only a few steps before discovering that this was not a journey to be taken in my bare feet. But my resolve had overtaken me. Nothing was going to stop me from venturing down that road either one way or the other. I quickly returned to the corner room of the cottage, slipped on my shoes, and again went skipping down the dirt path.

I hummed the tune my mother and I sang together on walks and errands. Mother could always keep me company with that song. Even when she wasn't actually in my company.

***

My walk began joyfully. Humming and skipping and journeying down the dusty lane. Within only a stone's throw from the cottage, the lane turned away from it. What lie ahead was not visible from Uncle Cheech's porch. I simply *had* to turn the corner and hope for adventure. And yet part of me feared what I might find. There was no reason for the fear. Only what I had conjured up in my mind. Perhaps it was another house. One with another child my age to befriend. Maybe it was more road. Maybe, just maybe, it was a secret doorway to another world.

I paused at the turn and surveyed the scenery. Clearly there were more trees. And for all I know, there may have been ferocious beasts that I was unfamiliar with. I didn't know Cyrandor at all. I didn't know what kinds of animals inhabited the place. And with the forested landscape, it was not at all unreasonable to believe I had heard some kind of rumbling, or growl.

And really, I believed I did. I didn't make a move. I didn't make a sound. I stood motionless on the dirt road. I turned my head this way and that looking for some kind of clue. Some kind of animal. Some kind of --.

***

There it was again. That rustling sound. Only this time, I knew its source. I glanced down at my feet and listened to them twist on the gravel beneath. It was strange how frightening, and akin to an animal, the sound of the movement was. But it was only me. Me and my imagination, once again causing my spine to tingle ever so slightly.

I rounded the bend and continued on my way, still uneasy in my surroundings yet determined to discover Cyrandor. And as soon as I resumed my journey, I heard another sound. One I had already become familiar with. The sound of the door on the front porch of the cottage. I heard Uncle Cheech's gravelly voice call out my name, with the tiniest hint of concern. He still spoke it as if he were calling someone much younger than I.

Nevertheless, the sound was comforting. And I could hear Grandpa in his voice too. And a little of my mother. I missed her ever so much. I resumed humming our song as I turned back toward the cottage and quickened my pace back to my Uncle. Cyrandor would have to wait for me a little while longer.

CHAPTER TWO

I couldn't believe I had been in Cyrandor for a whole week.
Nothing had happened. Nothing but that one scary sound.
Although, that's not entirely true. I had learned card games
from Uncle Cheech and I had learned a little about building a
fire and about kindling. Uncle Cheech was a good teacher.
But I still was uncertain what he set off to do every day. He
was absent most mornings when I awoke, but never gone long.
I had a few chores that he had established for me, and so I
hadn't ventured back down the road since that first day.

Today, though I hoped that would change. I had finished the
floors much sooner than the days before, and I knew that Uncle
would not be home for another hour. I became all the more
determined to retrace my steps and perhaps make it past that
bend in the road. And I did. And you know what I found?

It was actually something incredible, but I didn't know it. I
only just captured a glimpse. I was gripped with fear with such
a glimpse because I had never seen anything like it before. But
I knew about them. I knew about the majestic creature. I was
in awe of the way the sunshine glowed behind it though. And I
timidly approached him. He wasn't what I would have
pictured. His fur was a bright red, maybe an auburn, color. His
long mane was a little darker and shuffled in the breeze. He
was a beautiful horse. And his name was August.

***

Most people wonder how I knew. How I knew his name. I
didn't name him, and I never met anyone else around him. And
that's the fascinating part. August told me. He told me his
name. But not right away. No, that first moment was silent.

I was aware of the breezes. I was aware of the sunshine. But the sounds around me I didn't hear. I didn't even hear Uncle Cheech come back. I simply watched August grazing. I saw him whinny and snicker. But I didn't hear him. Off to the side of the dirt road was a forest of pine trees. And at the forest's edge was a stone fence or wall that was tall enough to sit upon, but not so tall that it was a struggle to climb. I sat there as I watched.

In that moment I was certain there was a lake on the other side with beautiful fountains. And the way the sun hit the water created a rainbow affect in the spray. And as the road neared August, it also simply ended. The road disappeared into a rolling green hillside. August stood at its base facing away from me. There were three little children playing near the lake, but they hardly noticed the animal that stood nearby. I was so transfixed on August that I offered no introduction of my own.

I don't recall too many details about the children. Perhaps they were slightly younger than I. It was as if they were building a snowman maybe, but my recollection of the morning was green and warm. I'll never forget that morning. For August grew to be my very best friend in Cyrandor. Though there would be others soon enough.

***

For a moment August turned his head. I am certain he caught sight of me, and perhaps he wondered of my own quizzical appearance. He did not say so. Certainly, he did not say so. But he looked my way and he blinked. And neighed, rather neighborly so. It was at that introduction, that I drew down from my perch. He neighed again and nodded his head as if to invite me over.

Standing at the base of the wall, I hesitated. Was it absurd to believe that August was inviting me, a child, to keep him company on this particular afternoon? And yet, being friends with a child is not absurd at all. He was already near the three others. Perhaps they, too were his invited guests.

And I thought finally of the three children. The ones I had only vaguely taken note of in the instant I saw the horse. I thought of them. And at last, I saw them. One was probably my age. Another was possibly four years old or five. The third, even younger. The oldest did not seem very kind. I'm not sure why. He held himself rather funny. He ambled a bit more than the others. And rather than helping them in their task, he instead seemed to bark orders or throw sticks and other things at the ground as if he were aiming at some unsuspecting creature. I don't think now that there was anything at all for him to be aiming at. But it didn't seem kind. I wondered if he and August were friends. I wondered if any of them were my horse's friend. And for a moment, I looked back at August. He was still looking my way. And he nodded his head again. I smiled and as I took a step toward him, I heard Uncle Cheech. I think August heard him too, for he snickered in a way that was curious to me. I knew it was time for me to go home, but I didn't want to leave. And August didn't want me to either. But Uncle Cheech was in charge of me – for now. I began to turn towards the cottage, and August turned back as well. I knew he was disappointed. Perhaps he was disappointed, like I was, that we didn't get to meet. But I think he was disappointed instead in me. I didn't like disappointing August. Not even then.

***

I did go home. Or to Uncle Cheech's home. There was nothing I could think of to stop me. Perhaps August's disappointment might have made me hesitate, but Uncle was in charge. What would I have told him? What could I have told him? So I went. And nearly two days passed again before I could return. Those days were important ones of course, but who could explain that to a child. Even me. Even Rosa. But Uncle Cheech knew. In fact, Uncle Cheech didn't leave on those days. It was the first time he had remained at the cottage day and night. The evenings held that familiar aroma as I drifted off to sleep. And the mornings were given to fresh eggs and milk, rather than the colder kind I had become accustomed to.

Just as Uncle Cheech never explained where he went in the mornings, he never explained why he hadn't on these particular mornings. I was happy he hadn't left though. The rains in Cyrandor were unlike any rain I've seen before. I feared the cottage might be swept away. But it wasn't. It stayed right in its wooded habitat. Just down the road from the friend I had just met. And just disappointed. I hoped August had not been washed away.

CHAPTER THREE

The rain trickled down the flimsy windows of the cottage as though it wasn't really falling as fast as it seemed to. Because, in actuality, it was a very hard rain. But it was kind to windows. Like they were old friends. I was puzzled by this just as much as Cyrandor had puzzled me up to now.

"Uncle Cheech?" I asked.

"Rosa." Uncle Cheech didn't use ordinary responses like "yes," or "what." He simply acknowledged me with my name.

"Where do you go every morning?" I wasn't sure if I ought to even ask, but I just had to feel as though some of the pieces were coming together. They weren't. And he waited a long time before answering. In fact, he waited so long I thought he wasn't going to answer. So, I began to think of other things. More things I probably shouldn't ask him. Like why Grandpa sent me here. And why wasn't Uncle married? Why didn't the rain hit hard upon the windows? Who did August belong to? And when would it ever stop raining?

"Just down the path and up the riverbank."

His answer surprised me. I didn't expect it, and he spoke it as if I had only just then asked the question, rather than several minutes ago. So, I didn't respond either. I waited. Calculating my next remark.

"I suppose you'd like to go with me sometime."

It wasn't really a question or an invitation. It sounded more like it ought to discourage me. And before I could agree that I would, he spoke again.

"And I suppose you will. Someday. Better finish your breakfast. We've got company coming."

***

I sipped the last of my milk, rinsed out my glass and changed out of my nightgown. Company. Uncle Cheech had never had any visitors before. Well, perhaps he had, but not since I arrived. And certainly, his cottage did not seem to invite company very often. There were few places to sit. And the draftiness suddenly seemed more apparent to me. I combed my hair and made my bed. I tidied around the little cot and upturned chest that made up my room's furnishings.

Uncle had the foresight to keep some firewood and kindling indoors in the case of an excessive rain. We were fortunate to get a fire going and in due time we were ready. I sat on the rug close to the fire as we waited. It occurred to me that Mother might have had a batch of cookies freshly baked for such an occasion. I could imagine Uncle's cottage smelling delicious if we had done so. But we hadn't. And I pitied our company. Not only for the lack of cookies, but for the rain they had to endure on their journey.

There was a knock on the door. And it opened quickly thereafter, before Uncle Cheech could even stand or shout, "Come in!" And nevertheless, they did.

***

"Hi, Daddy!" was the exuberant greeting that floated through the door as though the weather on the outside indicated sun high and birds flitting about. Myra was my cousin. I knew of her but had never met her before. She was much older than I and was working on a family of her own. In one hand, she balanced a casserole of some sort and, in the other, she held her father in a warm hug. Her father, by the way was my Uncle Cheech. I had forgotten that until now. Her husband was staggeringly handsome, and for a moment, I too had fallen in love with him. He had a winsome smile and soft wavy hair that was very tidy and in place. The only devastatingly normal thing about him was his name – William. I changed it to Hudson in my mind, so that it matched the rest of him. Nobody else knew of such a change though.

"You must be the lovely Rosa!" she greeted me, with equal warmth. "I cannot wait to hear of your adventures so far!" My adventures? The rain has thwarted any hope for adventure I have had for a while now. And Uncle always calls me home whenever I'm onto something.

"Are you Myra?" I responded knowing full well she was. I caught a whiff of the casserole and my stomach rumbled knowing that whatever was inside was far tastier than anything Uncle had fed me up to now. My cousin must have heard the noise from my insides for she gave a knowing smile and plopped it on the table as she gathered fresh plates and cutlery. The only moment of hesitation before the feast was a peaceful prayer of thanks, and we devoured our meal.

***

And still it rained.

Hudson and my Uncle took to the sofa and were engaged in conversation far dryer than the air inside the cottage. Though family for several years now, they were not well-acquainted. Myra was determined to get to know her young cousin. We sat across from each other, cross-legged on the rug, and embracing pillows as we chatted. There was something not unlike a slumber party about our visit. But I regretted having nothing of adventure to tell her.

"I remember growing up, here," she went on. Her eyes held an imaginative gaze skyward. The faintest smile graced her cheeks. "It was a magical childhood."

"When did you leave?" I asked.

"I guess it was a few years after graduation. I had met William" (she still hadn't learned his name was Hudson) "in school. He's a few years older than I am, you know." I didn't know. It hadn't really occurred to me. In fact, when I'm my age and they're their age, they're all pretty much the same age, as far as I can tell. "When he left Cyrandor for business, I married him and went along."

"I bet Uncle misses you."

"He never wanted me to go. But I think he has accepted it finally. After all, now he has you." I wasn't sure how to feel about that. I love my Uncle, and he has taken good care of me. I am happy to have him, too.

"I'm happy to have him, too," I said. "Did you like Cyrandor?" Myra just grinned. She gave no response apart from that simple gesture, but I knew in that moment that there was much more to see and experience. I found myself wishing more than ever that the rain would truly go away. And the rest of the party awaited its return on another day.

"Rosa," my cousin said warmly, "you are the exact likeness of your mother. And she was one of my very best friends. 'Savor every moment in this place,' she once said to me. If she were here, she'd say the same to you."

***

I awakened on the third day to the sound of rain. But only for an hour or so. Just after breakfast I heard a loud crack of thunder. And the wind blew something fierce. There was no history of tornadoes in Cyrandor, but I wondered if we'd have the first. The windows shook, the door rattled, and then it was still. There was no more rain. It had finally stopped. I looked at Uncle Cheech. He looked back at me, knowing I was ready to go.

"Better give it time to dry," he advised. And I intended to, but only the time it took me to wash and dress.

Myra and Hudson had left before breakfast and it was just Uncle and me again. I knew that the sun's appearance meant that he would go back to work in the mornings. And that I could return at last to August. I hoped August had been safe in the rain and wind, but after much thought I decided I ought to stay home one more day. It would be important to Uncle Cheech. And perhaps my mother would be proud. Papa too. I would stay and savor the moment in *this* place. In Uncle's cottage. In Uncle's company. For Mother and Father. And for Uncle and cousin Myra. And, in the end I knew, for me.

(Not to mention that perhaps Hudson would have been proud of me too. Gee, was he handsome!)

***

Uncle Cheech and I laughed that day. We played cards and made silly faces and equally silly noises. We shared memories of Mother and Father. We sang songs they used to sing. We were just silly together. I hoped such a day might have inspired Uncle to talk about his job. But he didn't.

It was okay that he didn't. I loved getting to know him. He had so much of my mother in him. And a great deal of Grandpa too. It was nice to feel like family. It was nice to know that if Cyrandor held no more adventure than I had already experienced, that family was quite enough. And that such adventure was good. And fulfilling.

I slept well that night. Much deeper and happier than I had since coming to Cyrandor. And I knew that, in the morning, August would await my return. And so, I slept. And I dreamt. And they were sweet dreams. As if Uncle had wished them so. And, of course, he had.

CHAPTER FOUR

"Uncle Cheech?" I called out tentatively. There was no answer. I opened the screen door and stepped out on the porch. The old boards beneath my feet creaked a little more than usual and I knew how they felt. It had been a long few days cooped up inside. The air felt a little different. Clearer, perhaps. I decided not to take the steps this time, and I leapt from the porch onto the ground.

Tearing through the yard and down the road, I couldn't wait to get there. I hollered to my friend that I was on my way. He couldn't hear me, of course, but I hollered it anyway. "I'm coming! Just you wait, I'm coming!"

"Okay we'll wait."

I stopped dead in my tracks. This, I hadn't anticipated. And I felt a little foolish. My route was blocked by three children. The same three that had been playing nearby when August and I met. The oldest was dirty from head to toe and held an old slingshot in his hands. He leaned on his brother as though he were the toughest kid in Brooklyn. Looking at his sister, the youngest, I knew he wasn't. She wore a pink coat and had bouncy blond ringlets all around. She held a dandelion and sniffed it daintily.

I didn't say anything, but I watched them.

"My name's Jasper, this is my kid brother Tony, and that's Lila. You must be the new girl."

"Rosa," I said.

He didn't respond.

"I...I live with my Uncle down that way." I pointed back the way I came.

"Aw Cheech's old place! Well any kin to Cheech is kin to us!" he declared.

I sure was relieved.

"Who are you heading to see?"

"Umm, a horse." I was afraid to tell Jasper. I was afraid to speak those words, and after I did I knew I shouldn't have.

A smile began to creep across Jasper's face. Not the warm, welcoming smile that had greeted me as kin a moment ago, but the kind that had made me feel foolish all over again. Then he began to laugh at me. Then Tony began to laugh. And of course, Lila too. But only because her brothers were laughing. She had no interest in the present as it unfolded, save for the pretty gold coloring of the beautiful weed she held in her hands.

***

"That old horse on the hill?" Jasper still hadn't stopped laughing. "That animal isn't worth the metal he's shoed in!"

I hated hearing him talk badly about August. I just knew, even then, that August was something special. No dirty, arrogant, child could have understood August the way I did. And certainly not Jasper. I didn't figure Tony could either. Perhaps Lila, but Lila would have to discover something other than a dried up old dandelion before I'd take to her the way I had taken to August.

I huffed past Jasper and his siblings and kept on my way. I kept on, but only walking now. There was an eagerness to get away from them and an eagerness to get to August, but I just couldn't run on, knowing they were mocking me. Chiding me for my eagerness. I was grateful they hadn't followed me. And as I continued on, I saw ahead of me where the road had ended, as it had before. I saw the wall where I had perched when I first met August. The clearing and the fountain remained, as well.

And there. There was that beautiful creature, grazing in the perfectly green grass, as though the meadow had arrogantly painted itself, portraying its most handsome features. I heard him snicker, and I caught his eye. This time, I paid no mind to the wall, or to keeping my distance. I slowly stepped toward him. Toward my long-lost friend. I am certain that he smiled. And he moved his head in a way that gestured me near. I was only a couple steps away now, and he turned, and completed the distance.

With the smallest amount of hesitation, I reached to stroke his mane and side. His coat was the most beautiful I had ever seen. As the wind blew, I heard him snicker, and the faintest whisper. It couldn't possibly have been him. But it was. He whispered to me. He whispered his name. And I whispered mine back. And he bowed, as the proper way to say, "Nice to meet you, Rosa."

I grinned. "August. It's a pleasure to see you again."

***

Our first ride was everything I dreamed of. Where the road ended is where we began. In fact, as soon as I was on his back, he cleared the wall and went galloping into the forest. It didn't matter where he was going. I knew I could trust him. I knew. The way Myra had known I would see adventure. The way you know about anything you're absolutely sure about. I could absolutely trust August. And he never showed me otherwise. We raced on, leaping rivers and fallen tree trunks. I whispered to him to run faster and faster. And he did. Each time, whispering back, "Are you sure?" and "Hold on tight!"

At last, we came to a clearing. The sun was shining, as it does on a crisp fall day. It was neither scorching, nor obstructed. It was perfect. There was a tree with a thick, low-hanging branch on which I sat while August and I rested. And I started to tell him how afraid I was. Not of him. Not of that specific moment. But of being in a new place, with new family. And a house. I was afraid of what might happen after eight months. I was afraid of what might happen during the eight months. I was afraid of never seeing Mother or Father again. And I hated to admit it, but I was afraid of Jasper.

August comforted me. It wasn't as though he talked a lot. But he was there. And he listened. And I knew. August became my very best friend that day.

***

He took a different route back. Or at least I didn't recognize it. But perhaps we were going too fast on our way out that it looked different coming back. Nevertheless, it did look different. Cyrandor had a very stately beauty to it. Once you're out of the forests, there are glistening lakes and fountains, with large pillared houses. There were perfectly manicured lawns, and the most magnificent gardens and trees. Perhaps not all of Cyrandor would be filled with unclean adolescent boys, laughing at your very existence.

As I remembered Jasper and his brother and sister, I wondered why he thought so lowly of August. Who could ever? Had Jasper tried to ride him? Had Tony? Or Lila? Had August ever introduced himself to them, as he had to me? Perhaps he had, and it was something they could not comprehend. One must be of greater intelligence to understand the depth of a talking (or whispering) horse. The horse, in fact, must be of greater intelligence than they could ever dream of being. What arrogant, insulting, pea-brained, puny, adolescent, feeble-minded --

And there was the sound of the screen door. And my Uncle. August knelt to help me down. I stroked his nose, kissed him goodbye, and headed home. Jasper and his kin were not there to interfere on my return. That was a good thing.

***

"I met someone today," I told my uncle over a bowl of mashed potatoes. He nodded in response but didn't ask anything further.

"I met a horse," I continued, trying to talk to him about it. I wasn't sure what I was going to say, but I wondered if Uncle knew August, or knew why Jasper spoke so cruelly about him. Still Uncle shrugged with little to add. "And some kids, too."

I decided perhaps he didn't want to hear about my adventure. Or maybe he thought it strange that I met a horse. So, I added the part about the kids. But only to conclude the conversation. Which wasn't much of a conversation at all. "How was your day, Uncle Cheech?" Uncle took his last bite of potatoes, wiped his mouth with his napkin, and stood.

"The weather was nice. I have something for you." He brought out two slices of pie that Myra had left us. Then pulled from his pocket a small box and set it in front of me. Before I could open it, he turned to retrieve a couple of forks for the pie and announced the contents of the box. "It's your father's timepiece. I thought you might like to hang on to it for now." I quickly opened the box and gazed at the small pocket watch. "I can put it on a chain for you, if you like. It'll be easier to keep track of it around your neck." Pressing the button, it popped open to reveal the clock part across from a faded picture of my mother and father on their wedding day. I didn't study it. I'd seen the picture many times before.

"Uncle Cheech, do you know August?" I asked as I closed the watch. Uncle looked at me through furrowed brow. But he didn't answer. "The watch is lovely, thank you. And yes, I'd love to wear it on a chain." There was a long silence. Uncle went about cleaning our dinner bowls and then sat down to his pie.

"August. That's the one that comes after July, I think. Or is it September?" He took a bite.

"It's the horse between them," I said.

Uncle chuckled. I'm glad he smiled. But he didn't say any more about August. Another time, perhaps.

CHAPTER FIVE

Uncle Cheech didn't like to sit in the back row. He thought it looked like his presence wasn't intentional. And yet if we sat in the front row we'd be watched more than he was willing to risk. So, we sat somewhere in the middle. The pews felt hard by the end of the sermon. And I would have slept like the other children if Uncle had let me. But he had specific views on that as well. So, I endured the stiffness of the seating and took pleasure in the color of the sunlight as it trickled through the stained glass.

It never rained on Sunday. Cyrandor, I noticed, took such a day seriously. Even Jasper was in church. And as cleaned up as you can imagine him. There were plenty of sopranos in the congregation. And they sang louder than anybody. Apart from Uncle Cheech, that is. For a man who didn't talk much, he sure belted out his hymns. Soon it would become a game to us. To see if I could match his volume. I'm not sure I ever did. But I carried a better tune than he could. He had opinions about that too.

"Hello, Miss Rosa," Jasper greeted me as I reached the lowest step out the door. He was on his best of best behavior. "You look mighty pretty in that Sunday dress!" I'll admit that it was nice of him to say so. But it didn't make up for anything. Nevertheless, I'm sure I blushed. I supposed I had to answer him at church.

"Thanks, Jasper," I replied courteously. There, I had done my duty. I thanked him. I smiled. I think. Where was Uncle Cheech? Of all the moments for him to have disappeared! I began to look around anxiously, when Jasper had the nerve to speak again.

"He's over there. Talking to my dad." I whirled around to see him through the church doors, in the aisle, near the pulpit. Jasper's dad was the minister? "Don't worry, Pop's just filling in this week. Mr. Blake will be back next week." *Not* the minister. Perhaps an elder. Or just a guy. But Cheech knew him. Knew the family, from the sound of it.

"Okay. Well, I'll see you around," I said with barely any intention of doing so. Still he was my neighbor, so to speak. And there was some kind of admonition about our arrangement that Jasper's father just spoke about. How unpleasant.

***

By the time I had changed out of my Sunday clothes, I had planned to go visit August again, but Uncle thought better of it. "Sundays are for family," he declared. That didn't bother me terribly. But Uncle was my only family in Cyrandor. And every day was for me and Uncle Cheech. So, what was different about Sundays?

"Rosa, did you listen to Mr. Sutton's sermon this morning?" I nodded that I had. "Good. He said some very important things. Things I want you to think about. Things I want you to remember. And to practice." He paused a moment. I was enjoying his efforts. But it wasn't my first time in church. And I had Mother's Bible with me in Cyrandor. I read from it almost every night. Almost.

"Well, the truth is, Rosa. The truth is. Well." There was obviously something he wanted to tell me. Something he couldn't bring himself to say. Or maybe he didn't know how to say it, but he pressed on. "Rosa, I want you to come with me tomorrow."

Sometimes, when I talk to Uncle, he listens but doesn't reply. And in this moment, there was no doubt that we were family, for I said nothing to him. I didn't know what to say. He had said what he wanted to say. He invited me to go with him. On his mystery journey. And I replied with silence. And for the first time, I saw him fidget like I do when my questions go unanswered.

"That is. Well, you want to know what I do. Where I go. You see. I'm sort of. I'm a. A groundskeeper. Of sorts. And. Well. Well, would you like to come with me tomorrow?" It had become imperative that I answer. I couldn't stand his misery any longer. So, I grinned and warmly accepted his offer. Knowing that it meant I wouldn't see August tomorrow, either. But Sundays were for family. And my family asked me for Monday. And I couldn't decline. As a matter of fact, I didn't want to decline.

***

Everyone knew Uncle Cheech. They dropped the "Uncle" part of his name, and just called him Cheech. But they all knew him. And respected him. They were all very eager to meet me. And I enjoyed the attention. They asked him about Myra and William and their health. And I drifted into daydreams of Hudson.

Uncle said he'd be awhile, but he introduced me to the schoolmaster, Mr. Dixon, who proceeded to show me around. "Mr. Dixon, do you know of the horse on the hill?" Mr. Dixon didn't hesitate the way Uncle did. Or mean old Jasper. He spoke up right away.

"Well, of course, my dear girl. He belongs to the Guardian. Beautiful horse. But well beyond his years. Doesn't do much these days. Can't run anymore. But the Guardian keeps him well-groomed. Beautiful thing, he is."

"Who is the Guardian?" I asked, ignoring other questions that began to swim about in my head.

"Well, you know. He's sort of our version of mayor or governor. Keeps to himself, mainly. Not a glad-hander, but Cyrandor runs well under him. Never heard anyone complain about the Guardian, myself. I suppose he's well-liked by nearly everyone. Never met him, though, quite honestly." Mr. Dixon seemed like the talkative sort and I began to feed his enthusiasm.

"Why can't August run anymore?" Or perhaps I hadn't. Mr. Dixon seemed confused by my question.

"August, dear?" he asked quizzically. "Run?" I realized my error. Perhaps Mr. Dixon didn't know his name was August. But was it a secret?

"Isn't that the horse's name? August?" I puzzled.

"Well, that I wouldn't be a-knowing, my girl. Know he belongs to the Guardian. If you say that's his name, then I wouldn't argue."

"Why did he stop running?" I inquired again. But Mr. Dixon didn't know that either. He explained that August was an old horse. Likely to die soon. Only Mr. Dixon didn't use those words. He said something about passing on, or journeying to a heavenly ranch. He said that August had been the companion of the Guardian for as long as he'd lived in Cyrandor, himself. But he didn't know that August *could* run. And he could run faster than any horse you'd ever seen. And I hoped that Mr. Dixon was wrong about August.

***

By the time we had returned to Uncle Cheech, his clothing was dirtier, as I was accustomed to seeing him in the afternoons back at the cottage. He brought me to a small shed where he showed me some of his tools he uses. I took special notice of a long oaken rod that seemed out of place and useless among the rest.

"It's hard to explain quite what its use is," Uncle replied. He wasn't awfully familiar with all of the tools in the shed, after all. He kept with two or three of his favorites and did his job the way he preferred. The rest were apparently the preferences of the previous groundskeepers. Or perhaps for some other station in Cyrandor. But I knew Uncle did his job well with whatever tools he favored. There was no mistaking the attitudes among the other workers. Uncle may very well have been in full charge the way they looked up to him.

Before leaving, I thanked the schoolmaster, and expressed the pleasure of acquaintance to all I'd met. I also gave Uncle Cheech a hug. I'm sure he didn't expect it. I think he was pleased. And I felt his whiskers tickle my cheek as he smiled.

I was glad that he didn't send me home ahead of him, though. I most certainly would have gotten lost. Because everything looked different coming home. Just as it had with August. But Uncle told me not to worry. That soon I'd learn my way around Cyrandor. And to remember that it was all still new. And it was. Of that, I was sure.

***

The remainder of the afternoon was spent like any other. Cheech softly grunted at my questions. He avoided them as best he could. And I gave up as swiftly as I had any other day. Uncle was not interested in telling me much. On the other hand, he did take me with him. And I met his friends. And I saw his tools. And I met the schoolmaster. So maybe my questions would win. Maybe he'd soon tell me of August. Or maybe he really did think it was the month between July and September. Which, of course, it was. But it was also a horse. It was my friend.

"Did you use your timepiece, today?" he asked me. I slipped the old trinket from beneath my collar and popped it open. I showed the picture to Uncle. As he looked at it, he brought it nearer to himself and sighed. "That's my baby sister," he said with pride. But barely above a whisper. He spoke it with the tenderness of an older brother, and the pain of loss.

"That's my mother," I agreed. "Were you there for that picture?" I meant at the wedding, of course. But Uncle understood me, just the same. And he was.

"I was the Best Man." His chest puffed up a little more with that declaration. "But your Papa. He's a good man. The finest. The Best Man, if you will." I smiled hearing him praise them. I missed them ever so much. I think that's why it's sometimes hard to keep such relics. I wiped a solitary tear from my cheek. I tried to do it discreetly, but I think Uncle saw. "And your Aunt Kelly. She was there too, you know."

Aunt Kelly? I had heard so little of her. I supposed she was Myra's mother. But I wasn't sure. "Where is Aunt Kelly now, Uncle Cheech?"

He drew silent again. "Well, let's just leave it at that, shall we?" And we did. Because I knew it hurt Uncle. I knew, because it hurt me, too.

CHAPTER SIX

As I sat on my usual branch eating peanuts and tossing some to August I asked him how old he was. He snickered at me, and I became somewhat embarrassed at asking him, because Mother had taught me never to ask a person's age. I thought maybe it was okay, because August was a horse. But I felt sort of bad about it. August whispered to me to count the peanuts leftover in my pouch. Twenty-eight were left. And he nodded. And smiled a bit with his large teeth. I guess he meant to tell me that he was twenty-eight years, himself. But sometimes horses didn't say it outright. Sometimes horses don't say anything, you know.

"Is that very old, for a horse?" I asked him. August pranced about and trotted over branches and in circles and demonstrated his youthfulness in a dancing kind of way. I laughed with him and agreed that he had many more years ahead. Mr. Dixon simply didn't know August the way I did. "Do you know my Uncle, August?"

He ceased prancing about, but his stance was still strong. He looked me square in the eye. Bobbing his head up and down he happily remarked, "Most certainly do, Miss Rosa."

I squealed with glee. "Then he *does* know what I'm asking about! He knows who you are, August! What about Mr. Dixon? Or Jasper Sutton?"

Suddenly, August decided to be the normal kind of horse. The kind that doesn't speak out loud, but snickers playfully. I knew he was teasing me. I knew it wasn't time. Cyrandor had taught me that much. Everything has its own time. But I was losing interest in waiting.

***

The next several days passed like any other. In the mornings, I'd go find August and take a ride. In the afternoons, I'd return home to Uncle Cheech. We'd play some cards or read awhile. I'd pester him for things he wouldn't tell me. Occasionally, I'd dodge Jasper on my way to or from my outings with August. Each time I'd ride with August I'd see something new. And the air seemed to slowly get cooler, as if Winter was approaching. Or at least the Fall. There were lots of rainbows in Cyrandor, though very little rain. In fact, I don't think I had seen a drop since Myra's visit. But the rainbows settled in over lakes and ponds and fountain spray.

Sundays came and went, and I began to enjoy Mr. Blake's sermons. He had a way of including children in his lessons. And Uncle always came home from church with a mission to talk with me. His particularly favorite stories were from Genesis. He liked to elaborate on the beauty of the land and the sea. On the vegetation. And the friendliness of the animals in the Garden. Uncle Cheech could be a tireless conversationalist. When I wasn't asking him about Cyrandor. And other things.

One Sunday, on our way home, I saw Jasper pass me by in a rush. He was running from something. And close behind followed Tony and Lila. Mr. and Mrs. Sutton stopped a moment to say something to my Uncle, before Cheech grabbed me up and began to run himself. I hadn't seen Cheech run before, but as I peered over his shoulder, I saw the darkness of thunderclouds washing over the church steeple. Cheech began to grow tired, I could tell, and I called out to him.

"Can you run?" he asked me with poignancy. I nodded that I could. He placed me back on my feet, grabbed my hand and we began our race to the cottage. We took an unusual route. A shortcut perhaps, but in all my journeys, I hadn't seen this part of Cyrandor. I didn't take time to study it. It seemed important to Cheech that we get home before the rain. And as we leapt up the steps of the cottage porch and through the screen door, we were safely inside. And the rain began again.

***

There was a familiar knock at the door just after breakfast. Before either Uncle or I could respond, there was Myra, casserole in hand, standing at the cottage door. And Hudson. And I think birds sang at his entrance. But of course, the birds would have hidden during the rain. Anyway, I definitely heard a *ping* sound when he smiled. Uncle and I were already engaged in a game of cards, but we dealt them in. Hudson was on my team.

Uncle led with the Ten of Spades. It was hardly an original move. Somehow, Uncle always ended up with that card in his hand. And he always played it first. So I followed with the Seven of Clubs. Myra nearly knocked me out with the Four of Diamonds until my rescuer laid down the Ace of Hearts. What a way to be rescued. He smiled again. *Ping!*

This time it was Hudson's turn to lead. He continued with the Hearts, and each time he played, mine beat faster. My cousin was his true love, I knew. But part of me wished he was devoting all those hearts to me instead. I could see why Myra left Cyrandor. It's truly an enchanting place, but if the alternative was a lifetime with Hudson, who could say no?

"Ha! King *and* Queen!" shouted Myra in victory. She slapped hands with Uncle Cheech and teasingly stuck her tongue out to me. Hudson laughed and came again to my rescue.

"Pocket Jokers!" he sneered. And did a victory dance, sweeping me up into his arms and lifting me high into the air.

As he set me down, he kissed my head and stuck his tongue out at Myra. I had a wonderful rescuer on my side. I wish he'd visit more often. Myra, too of course.

Uncle rose from his chair defeated. "I have never been good at this game. Come on, Rosa. Let's get the place cleaned up." He wasn't upset about his loss. If you ask me, I think he loses on purpose sometimes. But he was very matter-of-fact about it. So, I joined him, picking up the discarded deck and putting them in proper order. I glanced at Myra, desperate for an opportunity to tell her about my adventures. But she was whispering quietly to Hudson for a moment. I went back to my cleaning and started on the dishes from breakfast.

***

Myra had drifted into my bedroom and glanced about at a few of the books that were strewn on the floor by the cot. She picked one up and stroked the inside cover. She seemed taken by the inscription. I had noticed it before but couldn't make out what it said. It was written in crayon. As I wandered in, her thoughts were interrupted by my presence, I supposed. But I didn't feel unwelcome. She smiled warmly. The way she had when we met.

"I never could understand what it said," she explained. It made me feel better somehow. And yet also disappointed that I wouldn't be learning its message finally.

"Was it yours?" I asked. But even when she owned it, it had been passed down to her. She shifted her attention to the books on the shelf under the window. Studying their titles, she pulled on the spine of a book titled *The Gondolier*.

"This one was always my favorite," she said with a grin. "Imagine a raft. Big enough to hold a small house. And a handsome giant, pushing it upstream." She opened the book and thumbed through the pages. She paused on one and showed it to me. It was a picture of what she had described. Only the giant stood on the raft. And used a giant pole like a gondolier. I had otherwise imagined him in the water, pushing from behind.

"Myra?" I started as she continued to thumb through the pages. She nodded though didn't look up. "I had an adventure." My cousin stopped and looked up with a wide smile. She pulled me playfully down next to her wanting to hear every detail. So, I began. I began with August.

***

I told her about every ride with August. I told her even that August had introduced himself. That he liked peanuts but didn't eat too many. That he was twenty-eight years old, I thought, and that Mr. Dixon thought he'd die soon. I told her that he could run. That he could run fast. And that he always warned me to hold on tight. I told her that sometimes he would take me through the fountains. And that there was one clearing where we liked to go. And we would stay there for a couple hours sometimes, just talking and dancing. I told her that August can dance. Not a waltz or anything. But for a horse, ya know. He was a very good dancer in that respect.

Myra didn't seem surprised by my adventure. But she listened wide-eyed and intently. I didn't know if she believed me. But she listened. And other than August and Uncle Cheech, there was really nobody around to listen to me. And I suddenly felt kind of lonely. But kind of happy at the same time.

"Go on," she encouraged. I realized I had stopped my tale. And had forgotten what I said last. So, I told her that was all. And then I asked her if she believed me. "Isn't it true?" she asked, as if I had only that moment given her reason to doubt me. Of

course, it was true. All of it was true. But it seemed so
unbelievable, that I wondered for a moment whether it really
was. Or if I had only imagined it. And even if it was true,
would I be accused of making it up? Maybe I should tell her
that I had made it up. Maybe it would be easier. But I simply
believed that if anyone were to accept my stories as true, it
would be Myra. Surely, she would believe me. I began to smile
and nodded. And I think she did believe me. But it was time for
lunch.

I ate well when Myra came to visit. I ate well when it was just
me and Uncle Cheech too. But Myra was an excellent cook. I
asked her who taught her. Because it couldn't have been Uncle
Cheech. Perhaps it was her mother. The Aunt Kelly I had heard
of. But Myra didn't say. She told me the secret was in the
seasoning. But she didn't tell me which seasoning, either.
Nevertheless, I ate so much I was full. And I was so full that I
hurt. And I hurt so much that I laid down for a nap. And I never
lay down for naps. But as I slept, I dreamed of August.

***

We weren't in Cyrandor anymore, but in some kind of canyon.
There wasn't anything green around us, nor any trees. It was
unusual to see August without the forest around him or nearby.
But as we rode along, August was running right through the
river, against the stream. It wasn't a very deep river, but it
splashed all around us as we ran. The canyon walls were nearly
too high to see the tops of them, and the sun was intensely
warm. Warmer than it ever was in Cyrandor. From time to
time, August would stop, and we would drink from the river.

When we came to the end of the river, we met the sea. It was
fairly calm as far as seas go. There were no boats that I could
see, and there wasn't much of a beach. The water instead
pounded on rocks that stretched high into cliffs like the canyon

walls. As we waded out into the waves, I felt August's legs buckle beneath us, and he struggled to keep standing. He whispered to me to hold on and he charged out of the water and up one of the rocks. Stopping midway to the top, we looked out over the waters which maintained their calm despite whatever had interfered with August's balance.

He paused only a moment more and then continued up the rock, finally reaching the top. From there we could see out not only over the water, but also the canyon we had traveled through. And as August began to steer us back, from above this time, I leaned closer and wrapped my arms around his neck. He went faster than ever before, leaping canyon gaps and racing toward home. My heart pounded in my chest until I realized something was different this time. Something felt strange. I felt warmth. And discovered there was someone else on August's back as well. He had a familiar laugh. And he was clinging to my waist for support. As I turned to look behind me, I saw Jasper, jaws open in laughter and excitement. Not mocking me this time, but truly enjoying himself. But the surprise of seeing him made me jump. And I awoke from the start.

***

The cottage held that all-too-familiar aroma. The kind I often noticed at night. Uncle Cheech, Myra, and Hudson spoke in hushed tones in the other room. I couldn't hear them well enough to understand what they said. But I lay in bed imagining it was something secretive. Something I wasn't supposed to know. But I did. Because they spoke about it while they thought I was sleeping. I imagined they were planning something. That we would all be sneaking out that night to visit some old seer in Cyrandor. That he would tell us of the Guardian and some kind of dark fate that would befall Cyrandor if we didn't act immediately. Then, of course, we'd have to call August and the four of us would ride out—

But in reality, you can't fit all four of us on a horse. So, Uncle and Myra would ride another horse. And Hudson and I on August. And the four of us and the two horses would ride to the edge of town to notify the Guardian of whatever the danger was, but he wouldn't listen to us. And he wouldn't understand the urgency of the situation. And in the course of trying to explain it to him, fate would begin to take its place. Maybe it would grow dark, and there would be fewer and fewer rainbows. And the rain would begin to—

Wait a minute! What about the rain! It is just rain, after all! Isn't it? It seemed Uncle was almost afraid of it. And yet, it's raining now. What about that? Maybe, there *is* a seer. Maybe, there *is* a dark fate that awaits us! I need to get a better view of them. Or at least within earshot.

Again, I jolted awake. My dreams have the most vivid imagination. A dark fate, indeed. In my newly alert state, I knew there was nothing to fear in the rain. It was simply rain. It happened once before. Probably more than that, even. But it was still nice to think of August as a hero. And Hudson, too.

***

The next morning, I awoke to the sound of the remaining drops of rain dripping sporadically from the roof. It certainly wasn't dry, but for the most part, the rain had stopped. I joined Uncle in the kitchen for breakfast and said a quick prayer, thanking God for his company during the rain. It was nice having him home when I awoke in the mornings. Myra had gone home, of course, and it was just the two of us again. But another knock sounded on the front door. I was curious, but I let Uncle answer. I couldn't see who it was, but Cheech's greeting made me believe it was someone young. I snuck over to a window where I could see better, but I still couldn't get a look at him.

Just before Uncle closed the door, he said, "Goodbye, Jas."
Jas? Who was Jas? It couldn't have been Jasper, could it? And
if it was, why would Jasper be here? What business did Jasper
have with my Uncle? No. It couldn't have been Jasper.

"Who was it, Uncle Cheech?" I asked. I hoped and prayed that
it wasn't Jasper Sutton. The smelly, old –

"That was Jasper," my Uncle responded. What was *he* doing
here? He better not come near my house again or I'll—"He
wanted to know if you could come out and play today," Uncle
interrupted. Come out and play? Me? What does he want to
play with me for?

"What did you tell him?" I asked hesitantly. But Uncle had said
that I need to stay home today. That I could see him tomorrow,
if he wanted. But I really didn't want to. See him tomorrow,
that is. At least, I didn't have to see him today. But still. Why
me? Why couldn't he play with some other kid. Like his
brother. Or a schoolmate. Not me. No way. Not me.

CHAPTER SEVEN

As tomorrow rolled around, I headed back out to see August, but met Jasper instead. He greeted me happily, as if he and I were old friends. We weren't. I couldn't even fathom why he believed we were. Nor could I think of a reason I couldn't stop and play with him. He laughed at me the last time I told him of August. And I had never been to the river's edge before. He said it wasn't far and that he had some perfect skipping stones in his pockets. To be honest, I had never skipped stones before and I wasn't sure I wanted to learn today. But I went with him, anyway. And I hoped August wouldn't be disappointed. It wasn't as though I wouldn't see August today. Just not right now. Right now, I had to be neighborly. I had to "keep a stiff upper lip" as my Grandpa would say. And I'd have to make a new friend. Although, Jasper apparently thought we already were friends. I still couldn't figure that.

"You have to hold it so that it rests on your middle finger, like this," he said, showing me the smooth stone he was going to let me skip first. His thumb and pointer finger balanced it as he stretched back his wrist and demonstrated the throwing action with a swift flick. Then he handed over the rock. I took it in my left hand and tried holding it the way he did. "Naw, that's not it, Rosa!" he scolded. "Ya gotta hold it with your right hand! No way you're gonna get it to bounce with your left!" I assumed he was right, but only because I usually do things with my right hand. Uncle Cheech, though, was left-handed, and I bet he could throw a rock better than Jasper, any day. So, I decided to try it with my left to spite.

"Well, I'd have a better chance than with my right!" I shot back at him. I'm sure that wasn't very neighborly, but I resented him for dragging me out here to begin with. I began to wind my arm back and flicked my wrist just as I saw him do. But he was right. The stone plopped into the river, straight down to the bottom and buried itself into the riverbed. And he made sure I knew I was wrong. So, I tried again with my right. But Jasper was reluctant to let me use the stones he found, until I promised I'd use my right.

***

Again, I balanced it on my finger, and steadied it with the other two. As I stretched back to take aim, I flicked my wrist, released the stone, and off it went skipping down the river. I was so pleased with myself that I let out a holler and Jasper shot his arms up in victory. He was proud of me, I think, but more so impressed with himself for teaching me how. It skipped nearly five times before settling into the drink.

"That's the way, Rosa! Try it again!" And he handed me another. Again, the stone went hopping along down the waterway, and I reached for another stone. Six hops with that one! And a fourth stone. Six again! Jasper was reeling. Me too! I hadn't been so excited since August and I met that very first day. "Come on!" he called, as he grabbed my hand and began to run upstream. "There are some great skipping stones up this way! I'll teach you how to find them!"

It was funny. I didn't feel so resentful toward Jasper now. I knew it wouldn't last, but I was actually having fun. He was kind of like a friend, although I wouldn't go so far as to call him that. But it was nice. And I thought for a moment about taking him to see August. Maybe he didn't really know much about my horse. It's easier to laugh at people when you don't really know them. But I still wasn't quite sure. I thought I'd better wait, and make Jasper prove himself. Prove he could continue to be nice. And prove he could really be my friend.

We continued upstream until the river got plenty shallow. Jas rolled up his trousers, pulled off his shoes and stepped into the water. He told me to do the same, but I hesitated at the sight of the minnows. "They're not gonna bother ya," he reassured me. And I was beginning to trust him. So, I followed him into the river. "Here, this one's a beauty," he exclaimed reaching for a larger one that resembled the slate from my school desk back home. "See how slim and smooth it is? It's bigger than the really good ones, but it's fun to try them out!" I studied its texture and shape and began to look for my own.

Just as I reached in to examine one, a fish swam right under my palm and I yanked my hand out with a squeal. I hopped clumsily to the bank, trying to quickly leap out of the water. Jasper began his laughter again. The mocking kind that made me want to kick him in the shins. But I didn't. Instead, I picked myself up and stepped back down into the river. With the fish. And glared at Jasper.

***

"They're just fish!" he shouted. "Don't be sore. Look!" He reached in and caught one of the little ones right in his palm. He pulled it out and held it in the air as if that would prove they weren't slimy and that my skin wouldn't crawl from the touch. But it did. The fish dangled in the air flopping and contorting trying desperately to get loose and back in the water. I almost felt sorry for it. And no matter how much I hated being in the river with the fish, the water itself was cool and refreshing. And there was no way I was going to let Jasper win. I was not afraid. I was going to find the best skipping rock out there.

I tiptoed back over to where the incident occurred and tried to locate my stone again. I couldn't find the one that interested me before, but there seemed to be a heap of them a short distance away. I pulled a few from the river and shoved them into my pockets. I probably should have dried them first, or brushed away the sand. But I didn't. And I looked for more. By the time we headed back to throw our new stones, my pockets were so heavy I was practically waddling from the weight of them.

Jasper claimed he was taking us back to the same spot, but it looked different somehow. And I couldn't determine why. But I trusted him still. We climbed up the bank a few yards and sat down to sort out our stones. He tossed some of mine away assuring me they wouldn't skip because of this bump or that chip or some other blemish. But I still had quite a pile to choose from. And this time, he let me choose my first. He gave me a quick review on how to hold it and release it and I walked down to the edge. I pulled my arm back, flicked my wrist, released the rock, and there it went. I couldn't even count the number of times it skipped. In fact, I even lost sight of it before it stopped.

Jasper had a peculiar grin on his face. I couldn't believe what had just happened, but it was as though he wasn't surprised. "Attagirl, Rosa," he said quietly and affirmatively. It was a comforting tone. And reassuring. And friendly. And I forgave him of everything. And smiled with him.

***

I realized, soon after, that Uncle would be home soon, and I hadn't seen August yet. But there wasn't time to go now. August would have to wait. And I hoped he wasn't mad. But in all of our days together, I'd never seen August mad. But that doesn't mean it's okay to disappoint a friend. Even for a new friend. Even for Jasper. Even then.

"I forgot to visit August," I told him. Because I trusted him now. And I thought he might understand.

"Aw, that old horse? Why do you care about him, anyway?" It

still hurt to hear Jasper talk about him like that. But this time, I think he was actually jealous. And his jealousy almost pleased me. And I debated whether to tell him about August. So, I only told a little.

"August is a good friend. He plays with me. And listens to me," I said. Although I thought it sounded kind of childish when I said it. And in that same peculiar way, Jasper asserted that he also plays with me and listens to me. So, what did I need a horse for? But I did need August. And I suddenly wanted to tell August about Jasper. And I wondered if August would be jealous too. Because I think August needed me as much as I needed him. "You just don't know him," I rallied. And to my astonishment, Jasper accepted that. And even volunteered to go with me. I liked that idea. But I wasn't sure if August would. "I'll ask him about it, next time. I should make sure he's okay with it," I said without thinking. And I realized suddenly that I had spoken as though August could tell me yes or no. *Tell* me! August is a *horse!* And I was going to *talk* to him about it? Of course, I was! But Jasper thought I was absolutely mad!

But he never said so. He just shrugged and dropped the conversation. And I went home to Uncle Cheech. After Jasper got me back to the road I recognized, that is.

***

I was sure August would say no. I couldn't blame him. What would he want smelly old Jasper around for? The thought of it was complete nonsense. And I thought so too. Kind of. But August was really upset about it. He wouldn't even talk to me. I had become like every other citizen of Cyrandor to him. The kind that can't talk to horses. Or at least the kind that horses don't talk to.

At least, that's how I imagined the conversation going.

But what really happened was that August wasn't there. I couldn't find him. I went to our usual spot, and to the clearing in the woods. And he wasn't there. And I missed him. I wanted to tell him about the skipping stones. I wanted to show him the kind that skipped the most. I wanted to teach him how. And I wanted to tell him about Jasper. I wanted to know whether he knew Jasper. And whether he would welcome him.

Cyrandor had held many adventures for me since I arrived. And I somehow believed that it was only just the start. Only the beginning of what might just change my life. Only the beginning of my friendship with Jasper. And only the beginning of . . . something really, really big.

CHAPTER EIGHT

There was Jasper leaning against the porch, tossing twigs to the ground from the thin branch he held in his hand. I chuckled at the twig he held in his teeth and chewed precariously. As though it was what made Jasper the child prince he thought he was. Uncle Cheech I could hear inside, as he took to fixing a handsome dinner for the evening. I could see the puffs of smoke billowing from the chimney, as the late summer air had begun to cool the cottage, a little too much so. I had spent the afternoon running a few errands for Uncle and got lost on my way home. But nobody seemed to worry that I was later than expected. And by that, I mean that Uncle didn't notice. I doubt Jasper was expecting me, because I certainly wasn't expecting him. But apparently Uncle was.

Jasper was joining us for dinner. And Uncle was fixing lamb. Uncle had a habit of pronouncing the "b" at the end of the word lamb. So, when I say we were having lamb, I really mean we were having lamb-b. Nevertheless, this was a dish Uncle knew how to prepare. And we went inside.

Around the table were four more chairs, in addition to the three I expected for me and Cheech and Jasper. "Who else is coming for dinner?" I asked. But Cheech, in his usual manner, grunted a few names that somewhat resembled the Sutton family, and I had no need to ask further. I stepped into my corner bedroom and changed clothes so as to be a little more dinner-like. Instead of the muddied little girl with the broken strands of hair in her face. Jasper continued to wrestle with the branch as he played with the fire. He hadn't said anything to me apart from a "hello" that was wrapped around a chewed twig. But this moment he called to me around the corner. "Hey, Rosie! What's that card game you were ramblin' about before?" He had, of course, become the less than charming character I first met with again. There was little of the adventure-spirited friend I knew in the river. And certainly not the one riding August with me in my dream. He was butchering my name and using words like "rambling." I didn't answer him.

***

Again, Uncle mumbled something from the kitchen. "Dozy Joker High" was the name of the card game. I assume that's what Uncle said. It wasn't that he was upset about anything. He just seemed tired. And perhaps a little concerned. We hadn't entertained anyone since I came to Cyrandor, apart from Myra and Hudson. So maybe Uncle Cheech doesn't do this sort of thing very often. And to have Jasper's whole family for dinner was something else entirely. I offered him my help and wound up boiling potatoes. Jasper went back outside.

"Uncle, why are the Suttons coming for dinner?" I asked. Cheech just looked at me and smiled a tired, but happy smile.

"I like the Suttons," he responded. He had a way with ending the conversation. Or so he thought.

"All of them?" I asked. I'm not sure why I asked it. As the niece of a peculiarly Christian man, I couldn't imagine Uncle excluding one or another in his appreciation. But the three youngest Sutton family members had made me question their own likability at one point or another. And so, I questioned Uncle Cheech.

He stopped cooking for a minute and turned to face me. He took my chin in his large, unwashed hand. "Yes. All of them," he said with a smirk. And then it widened to a grin, "But I have my favorites."

I returned to my potatoes and then kindly set the table.

***

Dinner became an event lasting quite a number of hours. It concluded with a game of cards that I had "rambled" to Jasper about. I was partnered with him, not by my own will, but we made out alright. In the end it was the younger Suttons and their mother who excelled at the game. I'm sure Cheech and Mr. Sutton did their best not to win, but it couldn't have been very difficult given Uncle's history with the game.

The conversation that seemed to course throughout the evening was that of marriage. How Mr. Sutton met Mrs. Sutton. How Myra met William. How Uncle met Myra's mother. And betrothal. Myra, incidentally, was betrothed. Uncle had arranged for her to marry a boy who lived in Cyrandor. It was arranged from their childhood. When she met William, she was betrothed to this other boy. And when the arrangement was broken, she married William instead.

Apparently, betrothal was not uncommon to Uncle, as he too was betrothed to my Aunt. She was a farmer's daughter in the next county over. Grandpa arranged it with the farmer that the two would marry. But Cheech said, arrangement or no, he loved Aunt Kelly. And would have married her anyway. But he didn't say why she wasn't here anymore. And I didn't ask. And neither did the Suttons.

The Suttons understood betrothal but had made their own decisions about their engagement. Cyrandor had an uncommon practice of arranged marriages for a great many years, though now it isn't done very often. It seemed peculiar to me. But Uncle declared it a quite respectable approach to marriage. Children depend on their parents for a great many decisions. This could be no different.

But I thought it might be at least a little different.

***

After the Suttons left, I began to help Uncle wash the dishes and clean the table. He could tell I was tired, but I did my very best not to make a display of it. Nevertheless, he took the empty plates from my hands and ordered me to bed. Ordered, however, is, perhaps, not the correct word. Uncle didn't have it in him to order me. It was more of a suggestion than a command. And one I wouldn't have heeded if he hadn't insisted. Or, at least, if I wasn't very tired. But I was. And I did.

I fell asleep almost instantly when I climbed into bed, but, even as I dreamt, I could smell the familiar aroma wafting around the corner, as Cheech took his place by the fireplace. It had become a rather comforting air. So much so that it sweetened my dreams. And stilled my fears when I missed my mother and father. In fact, it made me to remember them. And to remember Grandpa. Even then. Even in my sleep.

That night I dreamt of them. I dreamt of the day Grandpa had brought me to Cyrandor. I remembered all of the sounds as we approached Uncle's old cottage. I remembered the smell of the fresh rain as we made our way inside and shook the drops from our hats and coats. I remembered Grandpa's parting words and watching him leave as I stood with my Uncle. And feeling a stranger to my surroundings. But the smell that permeated from the other room brought a comfort and familiarity back into my dream. A feeling that this stranger was family. And that, suddenly, the cold cottage felt warm. And a little exciting.

***

It had been awhile since I had seen August and I was eager to talk to him. As I awoke, I scrambled to get dressed quickly, so I could complete my chores and run to meet him. Uncle was, as usual, nowhere to be found and I was off within an hour. Maybe faster. The route I took to find my horse was not typically filled with people gadding about, so I hoped it would be equally free today. The one person I particularly hoped not to see was Jasper. He would no doubt try to make conversation, though why I couldn't understand. It was hard to tell whether Jasper cared to talk to me at all, regardless of the effort he put into the task. Sometimes, I could believe he didn't like me the least bit, and yet, by some unseen force, he was obliged to befriend me. In whatever he perceives as friendship that is.

I was lucky today. I made it all the way to August without even an appearance of the young Sutton. And August was delighted to see me. I was glad. For the last time I went to meet him, he was nowhere to be found. And before that, I had been so busy skipping those silly stones that I didn't remember to come to him. A lesser friend would have punished me for that. But not August. August was as forgiving as anyone could be. Perhaps it was the nature of a horse. Or perhaps it was simply August's nature. But it endeared him to me even more. And I, nevertheless, apologized for my absence.

His response was a simple one. "Think nothing of it," he said. And he was sincere. Although I did still. And I promised us both that it wouldn't happen twice.

**

There were so many things to tell him. So, I began with the stones. I showed him exactly how I'd made them skip, but we weren't near the water. The stones simply fell sharply to the ground. And August mocked me for it. But in the way that a friend would. And I was reminded that it wasn't like Jasper. For he can wound someone with his laughter.

I remembered to ask August about him, though I hesitated. Our rock-skipping afternoon had left a different sort of impression on me than our other encounters. But it was just one day. And I wasn't sure I wanted him to meet August. But August agreed to let him come, if I wanted him to. That decision, he said, was up to me.

I didn't worry about August meeting Jasper. I worried about Jasper meeting August. What if he didn't accept that August could talk? What if he didn't take to August like I did? How would it change my life in Cyrandor? Would Jasper badger me more? Or would he understand me better? And in the end, was any of it worth the risk? When Jasper was being nice, I liked him. To be honest -- and I told this to August, too -- but when Jasper was nice, I liked him *a lot*. August shrugged when I said it and I felt kind of embarrassed. But it was a shrug that seemed to say that he already knew. And in fact, it hadn't really occurred to me before.

***

Before I left, I saw the clouds begin to darken through the halo of the trees surrounding us. It wasn't an ominous sort of scene, but I knew that rain was on its way. And I had been in Cyrandor enough to know that rain meant a few days indoors with Uncle Cheech. I didn't want to leave August just yet, but he offered to take me home to spend a few more minutes together. He said he had something he wanted to tell me.

As he knelt for me to climb on his back, I sensed he was being cautious about something. And as we began the journey to the cottage, he curled his head slight enough to look at me as he spoke. "Rosa," he began, "Cyrandor is probably a little unusual to you, I think." I couldn't disagree with him. "And I'm sure there are a great many things you don't, and probably won't, understand. Perhaps even I am a mystery to you."

His words were solemn, but there was comfort in the sound of his voice.

"Our time together, Rosa, has brought me great happiness. And you will remain one of my very few, and very dearest friends."

I began to grow sad and a little scared. "Are you leaving Cyrandor, August?" I asked.

"I am not," he replied. And a drop of rain landed upon his nose. I saw him wince and felt a drop on my own brow. "I am not," he said again. "But I need you to know how important you are to me. When the rain has passed I will see you again. And we shall leave it at that, for now." His voice was taken over by the rush of his feet against the ground as he quickened into a gallop. I grasped his neck and leaned into him. August's words were not lost on me. I valued his friendship more deeply than any other. But I feared their conclusion after the rain.

CHAPTER NINE

The rain brought a familiar set of visitors the very next morning. Myra and Hudson joined us again and I was beginning to treasure these moments with my cousin. And of course, her charming husband. If I were to be betrothed, I should hope that Father would choose someone like Hudson. Complete with the wave in his soft, dark hair. And his piercingly blue eyes. And that smile. There was that chime again, right on cue, with the sparkle in his toothy grin.

Myra always did her best to entertain me, although I was officially the hostess. I felt like a little sister. And that was a pleasant thought. I didn't know any sisters. Or brothers, for that matter. All my life it had only been me and Mother and Father. And now, me and Uncle Cheech. But I liked having a sister. Even though we weren't.

She listened again to my stories of Cyrandor. Of August and Jasper. Of visiting Uncle at work. And she not only listened but joined in with my stories. It's as if she knew details I didn't recollect. Or perhaps she simply enjoyed embellishing my stories. But it was fun. And we would laugh and collapse into giggling little girls as we'd roll back on the rug unable to contain our laughter in order to remain upright. In her company I could imagine Mother laughing along with the two of us. And simultaneously admonishing us that it was way past bedtime. But of course, Uncle Cheech didn't worry about such things, and Myra was old enough to forego things like bedtimes. But I missed my Mother all the same. And it was nice to have Myra around to remember her.

***

As dawn approached, we hadn't yet gone to sleep. And neither of us were ready to yet. Myra helped me to my feet and led me to the kitchen where she announced that our adventure would continue. I hadn't a clue what she was up to, but I didn't mind. I didn't mind that the sun was near or that Uncle and Hudson had gone to bed hours ago and might soon be up again. I didn't mind that I might have no sleep at all or that we might not actually see the sunrise for the rain. I simply didn't mind. Myra was every bit of a sister to me, and I was not about to sleep and miss this moment. No matter what the moment was.

"It's all in the seasoning," she said again. I remembered these words from her last visit. I couldn't decipher what the seasoning was, but I had a feeling I was going to find out. Tonight. Or this morning, whichever it was. My insides were squealing with glee. My outsides were squealing with glee. I imagined that this is what slumber parties were like. For I had never been to one but heard of them from some of my schoolmates with older sisters. None of my friends from home had experienced one for herself, yet. In a small way I felt as though I was getting a privileged glimpse into the ritual. And yet it was a magical one that couldn't be matched by a regular old slumber party.

"And this is the particular seasoning," she imparted, holding a small bottle full of leafy bits. It smelled amazing, but I couldn't describe it.

"What is it?" I asked. I took another whiff. "Where do you get it?" Still I recognized the scent somehow.

"It's the root of a Heckella Bush. They grow in the southern region of Cyrandor. And only in the southern region of Cyrandor. The leaves grow on the root. They look a bit like a tumbleweed. Although they thrive on the soil of Cyrandor, they don't grow into the ground. And they are unmoved by the wind. They are also forbidden to harvest."

I was stunned for how could she have obtained some if it was forbidden? Was it illegal? Was she a criminal? And was it a very big crime to have committed? I was afraid to ask. But she could see my concern.

"They are not forbidden for you or me, Rosa. That's what makes us special." But I still didn't understand. Why weren't they forbidden for us? But I couldn't ask still. "We are allowed. Your Uncle Cheech, my father, gives us that privilege."

And suddenly it made sense. Uncle was the groundskeeper. Certainly, we were allowed to harvest such a seasoning! And so, we baked, adding a dash of Heckella Root to every dish. And breakfast never tasted so good.

***

I asked Myra that afternoon if she might help me to harvest a bottle of my own Heckella Root, but we were hindered by the rain. And before the rain let up, she and Hudson had left for home.

I asked August where we could find some and he was hesitant to take me there. But I told him that I was allowed. That Myra said she and I were family to the groundskeeper and that meant it wasn't forbidden for us. I even offered to give him some, but still he hesitated. Something was still weighing heavily on him. Our last conversation wasn't over. And that August's hesitation maybe wasn't about the Heckella Root, but about something else entirely.

"It's not because of the groundskeeper, Rosa," he said. I cocked my head inquisitively. Perhaps it was about the Root. "You were born into that privilege. And I want you to understand that. But the more you understand that, the less you'll see of me." But I didn't understand. Why would August have to go? I wasn't going to stop visiting him. He was my very best friend in Cyrandor. And what did he mean that I was born into that privilege? I wasn't even born to Uncle Cheech. I was born to my mother and father whom I missed very much. Very much. And suddenly, it wasn't about Uncle Cheech. Or the Root. It was about them.

"Do you know my parents, August?" I asked. And he didn't say anything. But he knew them. And he knew why I was staying with Uncle Cheech. He had to have known everything. It was everything I wanted to know. Everything. But I knew it wasn't time. Cyrandor had frustrated me with this small fact. It wasn't time. But "everything" was beginning to work itself out.

***

"I'll take you to the Heckella Bushes," he whispered after a long silence. Somehow it was comforting. When we met, August only whispered. And as our friendship deepened, that gesture became more powerful to me. The fact he was whispering about taking me to the south region of Cyrandor made it that much more remarkable. He knelt down, and I climbed on his back, and off we went. I'm not sure I had ever been to that region of Cyrandor, as I didn't recognize a single tree or house along the way. We followed the river bank the entire way, and I knew from the scent in the air that we were getting closer.

August started to slow to a trot and I recognized immediately the large tumbleweed structure of the Heckella Bush. They were as tall as my shoulders, some of them, though most only came to my waist. August ducked his head toward one and gently nudged it with his nose. It didn't move easily. As Myra said they don't move with the wind. Somehow, without taking root in the ground, they were anchored quite heavily to it. I plucked a leaf and offered it to August. He bowed his head to thank me and then savored the small green as he consumed it. I pulled the small bottle from my pocket and approached another bush. August stopped me.

"Climb inside," he said. "The strongest flavor is inside the sphere." I gently created an opening on the side of one of the larger ones and climbed in. It was open on the inside as if I could have rolled along as a passenger. But the scent was stronger, too and I began to pluck the smaller leaves from the inside of the bush. I filled up half the bottle before trying a different bush. I didn't want to leave any of them empty, so I entered many of them that afternoon for only a small harvest from each. But I left with my bottle full, and an eagerness to cook for Uncle Cheech that evening.

But before we left, I asked August why I'd see him less. Because I didn't want to see him less. And if harvesting the Heckella Root meant I would, I would never ask him to take me here again. But he told me that Cyrandor's mysteries would start to unfold more rapidly. And as they did, the mystery of a girl and a talking horse might also be revealed. It scared me to think it was something unusual, because I had grown accustomed to our friendship. I had nearly forgotten that it was something peculiar. And August assured me it was nothing sinister. But such a relationship had its disadvantages.

***

It's true what August said. That the mysteries of Cyrandor would unravel soon. They had already begun. And I knew it, because nothing on our trip back looked familiar to me. In fact, apart from the clearing in the woods where August and I would spend our afternoons, and the route I took to get there, Cyrandor never looked familiar to me. Every trip I took with August or Jasper, or even Uncle Cheech on Sunday mornings, I could never recognize one path from another. Or one tree or house or shrub or lake. Or rainbow. Cyrandor's landscape seemed to constantly change. And I knew it. I realized it. But still I didn't understand it. And I didn't question it. Because I didn't want August to leave. And I feared he would. The more I understood, the less I would see of him, he said. And because of that, I preferred the mystery. But it's hard not to pursue a mystery, when it starts to unravel. So, in some ways, I did.

I asked Uncle Cheech to take me back to work with him. I wanted to talk again to Mr. Dixon. I didn't have to ask him questions. I didn't even have to know the questions. He gave the answers. Unsolicited, and without further explanation. In some small way, I could understand a little, but not too much. And then, maybe, August wouldn't leave. And, maybe, I could have an inkling why.

If Uncle said no, then I suppose I could wait another week or two. School was due to start soon. Or so I assumed. It seemed about the time that schools start again. In some ways, I was ready. Maybe it would be a distraction to all the peculiarities I had encountered. And, maybe, I'd make some more friends. Friends who could be friendlier than Jasper. And, maybe, some who were also human, unlike August. But of course, August wasn't the worse for it.

It was fortunate that Uncle agreed.

CHAPTER TEN

The sky was almost purple when I joined Uncle that morning. It was pretty. I had seen it that color before, because Cyrandor had a way with that sort of thing. But it wasn't very often I was up this early to see it. Uncle talks quite a bit more in the morning than he does at supper time. He kept jabbering the whole way to his tool shed. That's where he told me to wait for Mr. Dixon. But he couldn't wait with me. He had to get started for the day. He collected a few long-handled gadgets from the shed and headed off up the hillside. I watched him as he went. I thought about following him, but I didn't. I stayed and waited for Mr. Dixon.

As I waited, I peered across the lake and watched the fountain in the middle. It reminded me of the day I met August. I must have gotten caught up in that daydream because I didn't notice the schoolmaster as he approached me. He startled me when I heard him call.

"Rosa? Good morning, little lady!" He noticed my body jolt slightly. "Oh, I beg your pardon. I dinna mean to scare ya none." He was a kind old man. I assured him it was nothing to be concerned about. Then he offered to take me down to the "crick," as he called it, and watch the world drift by for a time. It seemed like a pleasant thing to do, and I wondered if it would be the same place Jasper and I learned to skip some stones. Or rather, I learned, and Jasper taught. The memory, nevertheless, was a pleasant one, and I looked forward to the trip.

* * *

We headed there straight away without much hesitation. And I was right. I didn't have to ask a thing. Mr. Dixon began as soon as we stepped off.

"Are ya all set for school ta start?" he asked. I thought it must be soon, but the schoolmaster confirmed we'd be back as early as next week. Or rather, the other children would be back. I would only just begin. I was pleased it was to happen soon. But I wasn't particularly interested in the mysteries of school. I had hoped the conversation might drift toward more interesting topics. But for now, that's all Mr. Dixon seemed to speak of. There would be twenty-six of us. All in one room. The youngest was six. The eldest twelve. Jasper's brother Tony was old enough to attend this year, too. I wondered if Mr. Dixon would mind me bringing August someday, to meet some of the kids. But I didn't ask him. I didn't ask August or Mr. Dixon. But I wondered, just the same.

And then, Mr. Dixon said the most peculiar thing. I didn't expect it anyway. But he stooped down along the path, picked up a stone like the ones Jasper and I found, and looked up at me inquisitively. "I dinna hope you'll be missin' too much school, will ya, Miss Rosa? I'd sure be satisfied if you could attend regularly from time to time."

Miss school? Attend regularly? Where would Mr. Dixon get an idea like that? "No sir. I don't plan to miss," I said. "Too much," I added hesitantly.

***

And it was true. I didn't plan to miss. At all. I didn't understand him. And I was beginning to accept that. I didn't understand anyone. And I longed again to see August. And yet, I was tired of not understanding. Tired of having to shrug my shoulders and accept whatever people said, as though I knew they were going to say it. I began not to care if it was Cyrandor's time. It was my time. It was time to get some questions answered. It was time.

"Mr. Dixon," I began with determination. "Why would I have to miss school?" There, I'd said it. I'd asked the question. I was direct. I didn't falter. I said exactly what I needed to know. At that moment. And I was rewarded. I got an answer. Mr. Dixon told me exactly why he hoped I wouldn't miss.

"I jes don't think it'd be right. Nobody oughtta be missin' school, Miss Rosa. Even if you are--" he stopped. In my mind I begged him to go on. Even if I am what? But he paused a long while. And then finally, "Even if you are --- tired." Tired? That couldn't be what he was going to say. Do I look tired? Did he really think I was going to be tired? And that being tired meant I wouldn't go to school?

I thought back a couple years, to a day when my teacher decided I was sick, and she wanted to send me home. I just wanted to go back to my desk. And I cried all afternoon until Mother came to get me. Even though I was sick. But I couldn't bear the thought of missing school. I couldn't bear the thought of missing even now. And tired wouldn't cut it.

"Mr. Dixon," I said again. "Have other kids -- I mean, do people in Cyrandor get --- Mr. Dixon, am I ---" I didn't know how to proceed. "Have you ever skipped one of those stones, Mr. Dixon?" I asked feeling defeated. I took the stone from his hand, though he let me take it. And we continued to the riverbank.

***

"It's been quite a long while since I skipped any sort of stone, Miss Rosa. But I used to be able to send 'em quite a fer piece, you know. They'd go a-skippin' 'til ya jes couldn't see 'em no mer."

"Will you show me?" I asked, all the while working up the nerve to ask again just what he meant.

"I'd love to oblige, Miss, but I can't recall quite how." I thought perhaps he was hoping to distract me. To persuade me not to continue in the discussion of missing school. He must have felt he'd said too much.

And, for a moment, there was an unnoticed silence between us. Neither of us spoke or continued on either topic of conversation. To be sure, my own curiosity was at the forefront of my thoughts, but for Mr. Dixon, perhaps, it was remorse. Or perhaps he was only pausing to recollect his days of skipping stones. But I don't believe either of us noticed the silence. That is, until I spoke again.

***

"Mr. Dixon!" I said again with resolve. My tone startled him. Which startled me. And I stopped again. I placed the stone back in his hand and then went on. "Mr. Dixon, you MUST have had a reason to inquire about my missing school frequently!"

Mr. Dixon simply shook his head and responded, "No, my dear. I thought nothing of it."

"Surely you did!" I argued. And again, he shook his head and waved his hand in the air to dismiss the thought completely. And as if it were intended as one fluid motion he released the stone to begin skipping down the river. I'm sure he meant it to be a startling victory and again a distraction from the topic at hand. But in an uncooperative fashion, the stone merely sunk into the river like a rock.

Again, we were silent. And finally, Mr. Dixon turned to look at me as though he was at last defeated. As I waited to hear what he had to say, he merely shrugged, chuckled at the stone, and started back up the river bank toward the tool shed.

I was the one who was defeated.

**

I grabbed the stone out of the river and hurried after the schoolmaster. I intended to encourage him to try again. As I neared him I called to him, "Mr. Dixon, I--"

"Alright listen, Miss Rosa," he said turning around abruptly. "I shouldn'a said so much. And you're right to want to know. But it's not my place to say nothin' about it. But perhaps you ought to speak to yer uncle pretty soon, eh?" His demeanor had changed. He had effected a rather disheveled sort of mood at the river but now seemed relieved at his honesty.

"Thank you, Mr. Dixon," I began after a short pause. "Only. I thought you might like to try again." I held out the wet stone I had recovered from the riverbed. It was sort of a peace offering, I guess. And, nevertheless, he smiled and put the stone in his shirt pocket.

"Thank you, Rosa. I would like to try again." But he didn't mean today, apparently. He continued to talk of school as we neared the tool shed. Not about my not being there, but simply about what I might experience when I was. It sounded exciting. And I liked Mr. Dixon for a schoolmaster. So, I listened to his stories. And I smiled as though I wasn't thinking about everything I didn't know.

CHAPTER ELEVEN

As Uncle and I headed home that afternoon, I didn't mention my conversation with the schoolmaster. Instead, my mind drifted to the last day that I saw Mother and Father. It seemed like an altogether ordinary day. Grandpa was to come by later that afternoon to check on me, and Mother and Father would be gone most of the day. And they were. And Grandpa did. But when he did, he also told me we were going for a drive.

I saw the suitcase when I climbed in, though I'm sure he meant for it to be hidden a little better. We had driven a long time before I drifted off to sleep. By the time I woke up I didn't recognize the scenery anymore. And it was raining. And I was afraid to ask him where we were going. But he knew it was time.

"Rosa, I need you to listen. And I need you to be strong. Things are going to be different for a while."

"Where are we, Grandpa?" I asked.

"We're in Cyrandor. You're going to stay awhile with your Uncle Cheech."

I looked over at my Uncle, who was unaware of the memory passing through my mind. We hadn't spoken since we left the tool shed. But still he held my hand as he navigated the valleys and forests that marked our way home. I suppose, anyway. It still was unfamiliar. Even after three months.

"For how long?" I asked Grandpa. But it wasn't really important. I wondered about Mother and Father. I wondered if something had happened to them.

***

Still, I didn't know whether my parents were alive. Or maybe they didn't want me anymore. Or maybe they were being held hostage. Maybe they didn't even know I was gone. And what about Grandpa? I hadn't seen him either since he dropped me at Uncle Cheech's cottage.

When you're in that situation, you can imagine quite a bit. And I did. I began to teach myself about my circumstances. Grandpa was up to something. Nothing sinister, mind you, but Uncle Cheech was in on it. Mother and Father had not been taken hostage but were secret spies who had been called away on a special spy mission. They left me in Grandpa's care. But Grandpa was an even secreter spy than Mother and Father, so he left me in Uncle's care. And, perhaps, even Uncle was a spy! And he's in charge of training me in the family business of spyhood.

And, now, I have a directive. To spy out what it is Cheech is teaching me. Because when you're training as a spy, you're not to know that you're training. You have to spy it out. And if you do, then you'll be a successful spy. So just who does Uncle want me checking up on in my training?

I bet it's Jasper!

***

Having this newfound grasp of my reality in Cyrandor, I couldn't wait to see August again. And to discuss my theories with him. Naturally, he is part of my training. For how else could you explain anything as progressive as a talking horse befriending a girl like me.

I wondered if it was a unique spy-gift. Perhaps it is the peanuts he eats. There is something in the legume that evokes speech to an otherwise speechless animal.

Or is August purely an illusion prompted by the root of the Heckella Bush only available to those of us that are part of the special secret spy family?

And because of my spy training, I will not always be able to attend school like normal kids. Except when it is necessary for keeping a watchful eye on Jasper.

Is it possible that, at last, the mysteries of Cyrandor are beginning to unravel? Uncle Cheech continued guiding us home while such revelations were unfolding before me. But I couldn't tell him I understood. I couldn't give such proprietary information so casually to the realm of conversation, as we strolled home from the tool shed.

Uncle Cheech would have to spy it out and determine on his own that I have ascertained my role in Cyrandor.

***

By the time we reached the cottage, I was deep into my new career. Plotting my training. Determining my mission. Identifying allies.

There were my parents, but I wouldn't see them for some time yet. And Grandpa. I suspected the same for his visit. Uncle Cheech was my primary mentor. But there was also August, and, perhaps, Myra. Oh! And Hudson. I blushed at the thought.

I should like to apprentice under Hudson very much. And if I do well, he'll flash that smile I like so much. I wonder that he even might reward me with a kiss. And would I ever blush then!

I had to think no more about it. It was way too embarrassing. And certainly not fair to Myra. My own cousin! Besides, I could smell dinner cooking. And Uncle would expect non-spy conversation. Spies don't talk about spying, you know. Not over dinner.

***

I went into the small kitchen area to see if I could help Uncle with anything, and he shrugged his shoulders, mumbling something about the table. I assumed he wanted me to set it. I was already excelling at my new craft.

It was just me and Cheech, so it didn't take long to set the table. But I included my small bottle of Heckella Root the way you'd leave a shaker of salt on the table. I wondered if Uncle would notice. I wondered if it would add anything to the flavor of the dinner if it hadn't been added before cooking like Myra usually does.

And besides, if that IS the reason August can talk to me then I want to keep it in my daily meals. In moderation, of course. I wouldn't want it to make him too smart. As if all the words he used were incomprehensible because I hadn't learned them yet. He's supposed to be just smart enough for me.

"Did you have a good chat with Mr. Dixon today?" Uncle asked me.

I debated how to reply. I did have a good chat. I had a curious chat. And then, an astounding revelation. And an even curiouser walk home as a result.

"I sure did!" I said, hoping he would continue. But that was it. He didn't say anything after that. And I admit that I was mighty hungry. So, I didn't say anything either. We ate together in silence. Which was not unusual. For, you know that Cheech is not a man given to much conversation.

***

I fell right to sleep, that night. Somehow, I felt at peace with life in Cyrandor. I understood Mr. Dixon a little more clearly. I understood Grandpa and Uncle Cheech and August and Jasper and anyone else that had crossed my path. I understood. And I was happy. Perhaps, even excited. And I fell right to sleep.

But not before I smelled the comforting aroma wafting around the corner as Uncle Cheech settled into his chair by the fire. And, as I drifted off to sleep, I dreamt about the spy significance of his cigarette.

For, it was indeed significant in our line of work.

CHAPTER TWELVE

I was awakened hastily by Uncle Cheech in the early morning. It was so early the sun hadn't shone just yet. He told me to get ready quickly and to meet him in the clearing. He and August would be waiting. He was still drawing on the cigarette he lit before I drifted off to sleep.

I hurried out of bed and clumsily found my shoes. My hair was a little tangled, but it was easy to comb with my fingers. Throwing a hooded cape over my clothing, I dashed out as the sun began to peek over the horizon.

I hurried, knowing this was unusual and, therefore, important. And I hurried because I knew August would be there. But nothing looked familiar. I retraced the steps I took every day. Down the path from the porch. Round the bend. Past the stone wall where August and I first met.

But every time I turned, there was no stone wall. There was no clearing. I ran back to the cottage and began again. And again. And again.

Each time the landscape was different. It was wrong. I stopped once and sat on the porch. I went through it in my head and thought: perhaps, I've been wrong all along. This time, I went the opposite direction. The direction I remember coming from when Grandpa introduced me to Cyrandor. But it led to a dead end.

***

I turned back again and went the way I just knew had to be right. And still it was wrong. So, I retired again to the porch. This time, sobbing in a manner sure to become uncontrollable.

But it was imperative that I compose myself. I can't be a spy and a cry baby at the same time. So, I thought about Mother and Father. I remembered a time when Papa was lost. Papa didn't cry. Mother didn't scold him. They talked it over. And remained calm until they found their way. And so must I.

I knelt on the porch to pray. The way Grandpa had taught me. And Mr. Blake. And Mother and Father. Asking God to help me find Uncle Cheech. And asking God for the courage not to cry anymore. Because now was the time to be bravest. And when I rose, I wasn't crying anymore. And I walked back up the road. Toward the bend. And toward the clearing where I would find Uncle Cheech. And August.

And just like that first day, I did meet August. But Uncle Cheech wasn't there. And August didn't notice me as he grazed in the pasture. But someone else did notice me. Some obnoxious, rascally, villainous, childish boy. A boy who went by the name of Sutton. Jasper Sutton, to be exact.

***

"Well, if it isn't the youngest of the spy council!" he sneered, with that absurd grassy stick hanging from his snide mouth. I tried to ignore him, all the while keeping a close and watchful spy eye on him. Where was Uncle Cheech, I wondered. And how had Jasper discovered our secret? Was he, by chance, in on the whole operation?

He started toward me, and I resigned to the notion of responding. "Hi, Jas. Have you seen my Uncle?" I asked. "And what brings you out so early in the morning?"

Jasper didn't respond. He just walked right over and leaned in toward me. I didn't know whether he was going to shove me or hug me. So, I jumped at the start of it. And the whole scene disappeared. All of it. The path. The clearing. August. Jasper. The excitement I was feeling in the confusion.

No. Actually, the excitement remained. But the rest drifted away with my dreams as I awoke to the cozy comfort of my small cot and cottage. And I knew where Uncle was finally. He was just around the corner. Clumsily slouched in his chair by the fire. He slept there most nights.

Or at least that's what I always believed. I decided it wasn't the time to assume things. So, I got up to see for myself.

***

There he was, after all. Just as I assumed. His cigarette had long burnt out, and it lay close by in the ashtray. I picked it up to examine it, as my dream had suggested, it was a secret message.

Before Uncle had awakened me to meet him in the clearing I learned that spies would roll and seal secret messages. And the only way to break the seal would be to smoke it to the end. That would pop the seal and reveal the contents inside.

Unfortunately, Uncle's held no message. Unless he already read and destroyed it. Nevertheless, I thought it was a unique technique that I could develop and impart to the circle of spyhood. They would surely appreciate such an idea. And I thanked my dreams for dreaming it.

Before I turned back to my room, I had one final thought. I knelt down by the fireplace and used the poker to rummage through the ash and paper used as kindling. What if Cheech had received a message? And the evidence was here in the residue?

"Careful now, Rosa. The iron heats up mighty quick," he spoke in a voice not fully awakened. I had been caught and I didn't know what to say. But maybe Uncle would finally admit our secret livelihood. "Is there something you're looking for?" He asked. I remained silent. Was I permitted to say anything at all? Was it mine or his to reveal what we both knew to be true? "Go on back to sleep now," he said after a long pause.

And so I did. But only after another long pause.

***

I was up and ready for church in plenty of time the next morning. I wasn't sure if I was in trouble for digging through the fire the night before. So, I thought I'd be on my best of best behavior. And, at least at church, I didn't have to be a spy. I could just be Uncle Cheech's little niece Rosa, as so many of the congregation had taken to calling me.

Mr. Blake was preaching on something or other that I didn't find very interesting. I had a hard time staying awake. But I knew Uncle was keeping a close watch on me. So, I occasionally tilted my head from one side to the other to make it seem like I was really interested in what Mr. Blake was saying.

But, I guess, by pretending to pay attention, I sort of paid attention after all. A technique that might come in handy in the family business. But even though I paid attention, it didn't make it any more interesting than I first thought. Nevertheless, Uncle was sure to discuss it further on the way home. So, I listened. And of course, he did.

"Mr. Blake had quite a lot to say this morning, didn't he?" began my uncle.

"Yes. Quite a lot," I responded nodding my head as though I was still pondering all that he discussed. I sensed he wanted me to say more about it, so I fumbled through some chatter hoping I would land on something applicable to Mr. Blake's message. "I sure thought-- Well what he said about the... I'm just so impressed that God would---"

"Rosa," he interrupted. Fear struck again. In a way I hadn't felt before. It was as if things had changed between Uncle and me. I never feared him the way I did last night or at this very moment. "I can't for the life of me recollect what he was even saying this morning, can you? I think I must have fallen asleep with my eyes wide open!" He started to chuckle and there was a familiar gleam in his eye. I chuckled too. And the fear was gone.

***

"Rosa, you start school in the morning," Uncle announced. I got a sudden jolt of excitement. I loved the schoolmaster and I always enjoyed going to school at home. This was going to be another new and fun adventure in Cyrandor. And it would be nice practice in keeping an eye on Jasper, if that was my mission.

But Uncle confirmed it just then. Not outright, mind you, but the way a spy would confirm things secretly to another spy. "Jasper and Tony will walk with you for a while until you learn your way." But I knew what Uncle meant.

I couldn't wait for morning. I helped Uncle make an early dinner. And I cleaned up after dinner faster than ever before. On the upturned trunk, next to my cot, I laid out my favorite school dress to wear in the morning. It had belonged to Myra when she was my age. Uncle told me to help myself to any of hers that remained in the cottage. I often wore hers to church or when company would come. Which was only once. When the Suttons were here. But I loved the connection it made me feel to my cousin.

I polished an apple for Mr. Dixon and laid it with my notebook and pencil by the door.

But if yesterday I fell right to sleep, tonight was the opposite. I tossed and turned with excitement. I tossed and turned for what felt like hours. The nightly aroma of Uncle's cigarette had come and gone before I fell asleep. It was a long time. But, eventually, I slept. For a little bit anyway.

CHAPTER THIRTEEN

Morning came too early. It often does, but even more so on this occasion. I peeled my eyes open, though they fought back quite a bit. Nevertheless, the excitement of school revisited me, and I leapt from my cot to get ready. Uncle was already up, and I could smell fresh breakfast cooking.

I was excited, yes. But I was also nervous. I'd never been to school in Cyrandor. I wasn't sure I could handle breakfast the way my stomach was doing flips. But I sat down anyway. Because Uncle had made it for me. And he was excited for me too. "Are you ready for your first day?" I nodded and smiled with my checks full of scrambled eggs. I was careful to keep my mouth closed though. Mother had taught me not to speak with my mouth full. "As soon as you finish your breakfast you'd better run along. Jasper and Tony will be here in a few minutes." He handed me an apple. "Save that one for lunch," he said.

I took one more drink of juice, put both apples in either pocket of my dress, and picked up my notebook. I saw Tony through the window, and I started out the door.

"Hi-ya, Rosie!" greeted Jasper. It didn't even bother me that he called me Rosie. I was on my way to the first day of school. The first day of school in Cyrandor.

***

Mr. Dixon showed me where to put my lunch and gave me a choice of two desks. I picked the one I could keep a better eye on Jasper in. Shortly after I was seated, the large bell that hung outside the schoolhouse rang to signal the start of the day. It was a happy sound. Another beginning. Another adventure. A new Cyrandor for me.

"Welcome back, students," Mr. Dixon began. He introduced me to the class, even though I had already met most of them. Still, it's what teachers do to new students. And I didn't mind it. It made me feel kind of special. But he didn't tell them about my job. In fact, he gave me a different job. It was kind of like a decoy. But all the other kids had jobs too, so it made me wonder how many of them had spy parents too. Even Jasper. He was in charge of lighting the furnace at the front of the room. It wasn't necessary today, because it wasn't particularly cold. But it would be soon. In just a matter of months. Or even weeks. And, then, it would be time for my job too.

***

Mr. Dixon called me the Groundskeeper. Just like Uncle Cheech! I got to help shovel the snow from the walkway. And be sure the school steps were kept tidy and dry. I liked the title of Groundskeeper. And it made a nice decoy for my real job. I could keep an eye on everything happening in and outside the school.

And I felt a connection with my Uncle. And I couldn't wait to tell him about it. But only after doing my arithmetic. Because I enjoyed that subject very much. And I assumed it would come in handy. But in the meantime, I would have to endure the other subjects. And lunch. And recess. And continue that watchful eye on Jasper.

And I did. And I found that spying was kind of boring. Because it didn't seem like Jasper was up to anything. He was just acting like any other kid I'd known. But he kind of had this cool little curl in his hair. In the front. In the middle. Could I claim to have done my job, for at the very least, noticing that? Because I did. I noticed it a lot. And the arrogant meathead probably thought it made him look kind of cute. Which it did. But for that reason, it irritated me. A lot.

***

Recess was after lunch. And I didn't really play with anyone, that first day. I mostly sat and thought about August. Because I was tired of thinking about Jasper and his forehead curl. So, I thought about August and how I'd like to go find him after school. He'd probably want to know about my first day.

It was nice outside too. And would make for a pleasant trip to our spot. Or to the Heckella Bushes. Or down the river. And in my mind, I could hear the water as it flowed down the bank. But it wasn't the river. I felt a few drops on my shoulder and realized it had begun to rain.

The people of Cyrandor take rain showers very seriously. And I knew we'd be making a run for it soon. I looked up to see what everyone would do, and the kids had begun to scatter. Heading every which way toward their homes. And I looked for Jasper and his brother. But they were gone. And I suddenly realized everybody knew where to go and how to get there, but me.

***

I began to run. I at least remembered the direction we came from when we came to school in the morning. So that's where I started. I ran down the path. To the crossing road. Straight to the other side and down the hill.

But as I got to the bottom of the hill I had two images in my mind. I knew we came from the right. But the tree with the low hanging branch that we passed seemed instead to be to the left. And in front of me was another hill. I was suddenly in a valley I neither remembered traveling nor recognized from any other trip.

I headed toward the tree as it represented the only thing familiar to the morning's journey. And as I neared it I was certain again that I was wrong. I had to start thinking like my mother and father. I had to start thinking like Uncle Cheech. I had to be the "Groundskeeper" that I was and determine a solution to my overwhelming feeling of confusion and peril.

So, I climbed the tree. Perhaps with some height and perspective I could locate a landmark. Or a route home. Or Jasper. Or Tony. Or August.

***

As I neared a height that didn't frighten me, but gave me a view, I was awestruck. The hill I met as I descended the hill from the school had shifted. And the valley I didn't recognize was replaced by the river where Jasper taught me to skip stones. And, as I watched, so did the river disappear. And there before me was a forest for my tree. And the rain began to come down even harder until I could no longer keep my eyes open.

I sat down on the branch and cried. Leaning my back against the trunk and hugging my knees to my chest, I feared the world I had come to call home. I suddenly understood the rush to safety. But I could not fathom how I would ever find it again on my own. I was alone. In Cyrandor. For the first time in three months. And not even my spy heritage could save me. I had only one solution. And that was to pray.

And as I spoke the words: "Dear God," he must have heard me. Because I don't remember anything beyond that. I simply drifted off to sleep. On the branch. In the tree. In the rain.

CHAPTER FOURTEEN

When I awoke it was dark out, and the rain persisted. Though not quite as hard as when I had fallen asleep. And I was cold. And wet. And still alone in a tree.

I stood again on the branch to see if I could see anything in the nighttime. Even through the rain. But all was little more than a silhouette. Not of a forest, mind you. But of large spherical formations. And another lone tree. Though quite a bit smaller than the one I stood in.

Though still somewhat gripped with fear, I had a new resolve. I slowly made my way down the tree to the earth again. It sank a bit beneath my feet. And I dared not stand idle too long. So, I made my way in the dark to the spheres. I could smell them as I got closer and I knew I had found the Heckella Bushes.

I devised a plan to wait out the night inside. But as I passed the smaller tree on my way to the first bush, I noticed something familiar about it too. It was an apple tree. But not like we have back home. This one had a different variety of apple. You might call them candy apples. Or at least I did. And they were. And I picked one. And climbed inside the Heckella Bush. And there I fell asleep again. Only to be awakened by a peculiar sound a few hours later.

***

In the midst of the cluster of thuds, I heard a sharp whistle and a "Hyah!" It gave me a start. I peered out from the bush to an overwhelming silence. The sound was gone again, and nothing was in sight. Not even the candy apple tree. Or the bigger tree I slept in when the rain began.

I returned to the bush's interior. This time I heard a raspy, childlike "Hello" and the thrashing sound of a stick whipping through the air. Again, I peered out of the bush. Nothing.

"Rosa?"

I recognized that voice for sure as my cousin Myra! "Myra!" I called back as I poked my head out again. I could see a figure on a horse and heard a snicker as the rain began to pound harder once again.

"Rosa!" called the figure on the horse. Followed by a faint whisper of the same from the horse. August had come to find me. But he had help. From someone. It was not Myra. Nor was it a girl. Or a child with a raspy voice. It seemed again to be the whistler, this time.

Disregarding the rain, I locked eyes on August. Careful not to lose sight of him as once again the landscape seemed to shift. Between us was approaching another large mound of earth and I leapt from the bush to get to the top of the hill. And to not lose sight of the horse. Or what appeared to be Uncle Cheech.

***

"Uncle Cheech!" I cried as I ran to the summit. "Uncle Cheech!" between tears of fear and joy.

"Rosa," whispered August from behind me. I didn't see them anymore and I turned around toward the direction of his voice. At the base of the hill the Heckella Bushes had gone. But there stood my Uncle and August. As I ran to meet them, I could hear voices behind me.

"Come to me quick!" shouted my Uncle and he hoisted me up on August. August reared up with the two of us and whispered how happy he was that they found me. Uncle caressed August's neck and responded, "Me too, Gunderson."

As we started home I could see two others nearing the cottage before us. From a distance I knew the one was Myra. And I began to recognize the child as Jasper. They waited on the porch with William who was much dryer than the rest of us.

***

The rain had let up slightly as we dismounted and said goodbye to August until after the rain.

"You're a good steed, Gunderson," said my Uncle, again caressing his neck and kissing his nose. "Thanks for your help tonight. I mightn't have found her without you." I watched Uncle interact with the horse I'd known for three months as August. I watched August interact with my Uncle as though they were old friends. And he didn't seem thrown by the name Gunderson. But neither was I. Really. "I'll leave you with Rosa for a moment. But be sure she makes it inside before you leave," he said with a wink, as the dampness of the air dropped down his cheek.

I stood with August as Uncle Cheech and Myra and William and Jasper disappeared into the cottage. And then I spoke. "August?"

He nodded.

"Am I really a spy?"

***

"You're a Groundskeeper," he said with a wink. I smirked back at him. I was proud of that anyway.

"Is your name really Gunderson?" I asked. And to my Uncle he was. For August was a great many things to a great many people. To me, he was my friend. He was August. And he would always be August.

"Is Hudson really Myra's husband?" I asked, hoping for a loophole in which I might be his betrothed.

"Myra's husband is William," he responded with another wink. "And both of them are inside waiting for you." And he meant both William and Hudson. But I didn't realize that. At the time, I assumed he was speaking of William and Myra. And perhaps it's a little confusing even now. I had one last question for August before I went inside.

"August, why am I in Cyrandor?"

"Rosa. You are a Groundskeeper. " And he walked away with a cheery snicker in his teeth. And I went inside. And dried off.

***

"Rosa, I'm sorry," Jasper said, as soon as I walked in. "When it started to rain I took off. I grabbed Tony, but I didn't think."

"It's okay, Jasper," I said. And it was. It was scary. And I was cold and wet. But I also found that, at last, I was onto something.

"I'm just grateful for you and Myra and Gunderson," nodded my Uncle in Jasper's direction. "You were a great hunter. And you helped find her. We couldn't have done it without you.

"Your folks will want you back home in the morning. I'll see that Gunderson gets you there safely, if that rain hasn't let up by then."

Once we were all dried off it was time for bed. Well past time for bed, in fact. Uncle always tucked me in, but he tucked a little tighter tonight. And Myra and Hudson looked on with a special gleam in their eyes. As Uncle left, Myra went with him to set up a make-shift bed for Jasper. Hudson came in and sat down next to me.

"Don't you give us a scare like that again. We were all very worried," he said. I was worried too. But I couldn't say so. I couldn't bring myself to say anything.

Except, "Okay." And he cracked a sudden smile. And there went those bells right along with it. And, before he stood to leave, he stopped and kissed my forehead. And it hadn't been a bad day, after all.

CHAPTER FIFTEEN

It was still raining when I awoke. I could hear Myra, Hudson, and Uncle in the kitchen. Myra was making breakfast. And I was immediately hungry for it. Breakfast was never so good as when Myra makes it. I didn't hear Jasper. But I secretly hoped he hadn't left yet. And I secretly hoped that I hadn't secretly hoped that.

I changed clothes before breakfast this morning, because of all the extra people. And I headed out of my little room to find Jasper still asleep on the couch. I smiled to myself. And then shook my head in disgust at myself. And then remembered Hudson's kiss from last night. And smiled to myself again. And stepped into the kitchen.

"There she is," greeted my cousin. Hudson winked in my direction. Uncle didn't speak. Not because he was upset or anything. But just because that was Uncle Cheech. He never has much to say, you know. I sat down across from Hudson and next to Uncle. A few minutes later, Jasper joined us. The curl that is usually on his forehead, stood straight up. And there was a dented line down his face that hadn't yet worked itself out in his awakened state. His disheveled look pleased me. And I smiled once again.

***

Mrya set out five plates filled with potatoes and eggs and pancakes. And Heckella Root of course. And she winked at me, as I returned a knowing smile. Jasper began to dig right in, before Uncle could bless the food. Hudson reached for his hand and Myra's to remind him. We didn't usually hold hands for the blessing, but I suddenly regretted sitting across from Hudson rather than next to him. But I reluctantly took Jasper's hand. And Uncle's. And we prayed.

And Uncle thanked God for my safety. And asked for Jasper's on his way home this morning. And I involuntarily gave a gentle squeeze to Jasper's hand in agreement. And rolled my eyes at myself.

Uncle told me to stay in with Myra today. She called it a "girls day" and that sounded fun to me. Plus, I had so much to tell her. Even though she probably knew most of it. Uncle and William (because, of course, that's what Uncle calls him) would see to it that Gunderson could get Jasper home. And they would be back before dark. Or what "dark" usually is on a non-rainy day. Because, on rainy days, all day felt like "dark".

And before they left, and before Myra and I had our day, we all had our breakfast. And it was delicious.

***

Myra showed me how to make a blueberry pie. Because, of all the pies, she said, the blueberry is extraordinary with the Heckella Root. So that's what we made. And she was right. But to be honest, I hadn't tried any other pies with Heckella Root. Still, I couldn't imagine anything tastier.

"Did you have a horse friend growing up, Myra?" I asked. She nodded. "Was it a girl horse or a boy horse?" It was a boy. "What was his name?" I queried. And Myra just smiled. "Come on, Myra! What was his name?" I asked impatiently.

"I know what you're thinking, Rosa," said my cousin. "Gunderson and August are one and the same. In fact, even Grandpa knew him. And his Grandpa. August is a very special horse, Rosa."

I paused to take that in. Meanwhile, another bite of blueberry pie contributed to my silence. Finally, "and what did you call him, Myra?" I may have started to sound irritated, but I wasn't.

Myra just smiled again. "I'll introduce you if we meet again," she said. And I made it my job to guarantee that introduction. The only problem was that Myra would be gone again when the rain was over. And I couldn't go see August until the rain had stopped. And I thought for a moment and my eyes lit up with an idea.

I'll just ask August.

***

After the pie, Myra suggested a game of Dozy Joker. I had become pretty good at that, so I was eager to beat her at it. Before we could play, though, she had another idea. She grabbed my hand and whisked me out the door onto the porch. The rain was still coming down pretty hard. She stopped for a moment and then walked to the side and peered around toward the back of the house. It was wooded in the back and, therefore, usually very dark. I didn't venture behind the house too often. Or ever, really. But she told me we were going to make a run for it.

"In the rain?" I asked, remembering what I had recently experienced. But she assured me we'd be okay. But we needed to be quick. The richest mud was in the back of the cottage.

The richest mud? My cousin was as much a mystery as Cyrandor sometimes. But I trusted her. So, I agreed. She counted down, and we ran. There was a slight awning in the back that shielded us from the rain. And hanging on a hook on the back porch was a small spade. And another long-handled something like I had seen in Uncle's tool shed.

Myra reached for the spade and told me to stay on the porch. I did. And the spy instincts in me began to memorize the landscape. And I watched closely to see it change. Even subtly. For a moment, I got distracted as Myra leapt from the porch into the rain and began to scoop up the soggy earth. She again darted back to the porch.

"Here," she dumped the mud into my unsuspecting hands. I was beginning to lose trust in her. Perhaps, the rain had gotten to her. Perhaps, she'd gone mad. And then she proved it. She took my hands with the glob of mud and plopped them on my face and began to smear it around. I felt some of my hairs glob to my face with the mud. And I gave her a confused look. "Myra!"

***

She began to laugh, almost uncontrollably. She really had gone mad. But so had I. I laughed too. I couldn't help myself. I managed to squeak out the words, "Why am I wearing mud?"

When we both had finally regained our composure, she explained that the minerals in the earth were great for the skin. Especially the earth in Cyrandor. Of course, they were. And she made herself a glob of mud as well. And we went inside for it to dry. And to play some cards. And to laugh some more. And I asked again.

"Myra, what was the name of your horse?"

She laughed. "Alright, I'll tell you. But you'll have to promise not to tell William. He doesn't know about my horse. And he might get confused." I promised. "His name was...Horace."

Horace? Horace the Horse? Was she joking? August just doesn't look like a Horace. And Horace is something a child would name a horse. Like naming a bunny Bernie. Or a kitty Katy. Or a puppy Pappy. But she wasn't joking. She actually called him Horace.

"Did you name him?" I asked. And of course, she didn't. That's how he introduced himself. And I was starting to get really good at this spying thing. Excuse me. Groundskeeper, I mean.

***

As we finished our game the mud had dried stiff and Myra said it was time to rinse it off. I started toward the sink, but Myra had another idea. Again, she whisked me outside. In the rain. And it started not to feel so scary. We went around back again. To be safe, she said. Which sounded good, but didn't make any sense.

The hard part about going around back is that the cottage has no back door. So, it takes longer to get there. But it really is very pretty. And not as scary as I originally thought. Though it was starting to get darker. And I could be easily persuaded of its danger as well. But I thought better of it. So, we went to the back.

I was eager to see what the landscape appeared as, this time. I wanted to know if a hill moved in. Or a lake. I was eager to see it from the safety of the porch. I had no desire to be lost in it. But it remained unchanged. It was still the wooded landscape from several hours ago.

Myra stepped off the porch into the rain and reached out her hand to me. I stepped off too. We both glanced skyward and let the rain pour onto our faces. It felt refreshing. And messy. And I liked it. We stood in the rain. In the safety of the back yard. With a closeness to the back porch. And smiles on our faces. For several minutes. Enough to be soaked through when we went back inside. But as we rounded the front corner of the house, I peeked behind me. It had gotten pretty dark. Dark enough to be a normal non-rainy-day dark. And Uncle and Hudson should be home soon.

But what intrigued me is what I saw in the back yard as I looked behind me. Just before Myra hoisted me back onto the front porch, I saw a small piece of a rainbow. In the woods. In the dark. Behind the house.

***

By the time we had changed into dry clothes, Uncle Cheech and Hudson had returned and were enjoying a slice of blueberry pie. Gunderson was able to return Jasper to his family. And my uncle seemed much more at ease as we started on dinner. We were all very tired. And there wasn't much conversation that evening. I told of our adventure. But I didn't mention the rainbow.

Uncle grunted in his usual manner. Myra smiled as I recounted the day. And Hudson too. And I could almost hear the bells. If it weren't for the bits of food that showed in his teeth when he did. Still, he was handsome. And I was glad to have them all back.

We settled in early and I fell asleep before my head hit the pillow. The scent of Uncle's nightly cigarette never reached me. Perhaps, because I was asleep too quick. Or, perhaps, because he didn't smoke it. And if he didn't smoke it, perhaps, it was because there was a message in it for somebody else. And he didn't want to intercept. And I couldn't suppose it was meant for me.

CHAPTER SIXTEEN

As I awoke, I could hear the last few drops of rain as they journeyed down the window pane and dripped from the trees outside. I assumed Myra and Hudson had already left. But I could still smell the scent of Myra's breakfast, and I was glad she had left some for me.

I didn't hurry, but I dressed for breakfast. And, maybe, for school. And headed to the kitchen. I was surprised to see my cousin seated at the table.

"You're still here!" I exclaimed. She didn't want to leave without saying goodbye. She said I had become more like a sister than a cousin to her. And she'd miss me until next time. I felt the same. And I was glad she stayed. But soon Hudson appeared in the doorway with one final bag.

"We'd better head on," he stated matter-of-factly. Myra gave me one more hug, as Hudson extended his arms as well. And I hugged them both at the same time. I heard a kiss between the two above me. And then felt one atop my head, as we all let go. "Take care of your Uncle Cheech now, you hear me?" he said. Again, with the smile. And I nodded that I would. But it was something adults say to kids, you know. Of course, it would be Uncle taking care of me. But I was learning. And soon I would be able to. If I needed to.

Uncle and I waved goodbye from the porch, as they left. And it felt good to be a part of their departure. Because, always before, I had awakened, and they were gone. When they were out of sight, Uncle's arm that was around my shoulders, squeezed me in tight. And we walked back into the house.

"It looks like the rain is past us. You'll go back to school in the morning."

***

"May I go visit August this afternoon?" I asked. And Uncle said I could. But I had to first finish my chores. And help tidy the kitchen. So, I did. And I went. And August was there in the pasture. Grazing like the day we met. The fountain reflected the sunshine as though there hadn't been any rain at all.

I decided not to approach him, though I'm sure he knew I was there. Instead, I climbed onto the wall where I sat on the first day. And I watched him. He had become my very best friend in Cyrandor. He had been for some time. And I always knew there was something mysterious about him. Perhaps he gave it away when he spoke to me. And there was always something he was holding back.

He snickered and bounced his head enjoying the sunshine. Or, perhaps, knowing I was behind him. I smiled at how his coat seemed to glisten in the daylight. I had missed the daylight, these past few days.

"Look at the rainbow," he whispered. Though I could hear him from my perch. I observed the lake and fountain and the colors that the light produced in its spray.

"It's pretty," I said softly to myself. But I knew August could hear me. He bounced again and trotted over to me. As he kneeled I climbed up on him and held on. I knew he was going to run fast today.

***

And he did run fast. And I held on as tight as I could, though I could feel my hands slipping from time to time. And, even so, every time he whispered "Faster?" I clutched him tighter and leaned into his neck and gave my okay.

It didn't take quite as long as normal to get to our clearing in the woods. The spot we usually stopped to rest and snack and talk. August knelt for me to get down and I climbed onto a low-hanging branch just as I had done so often before. I opened my bag of peanuts and tossed him a few. He bit at a fly as he swallowed the peanuts.

"So your name is also Horace?" I asked.

"My name is August, which you well know, Rosa," he responded.

"But it was Horace?"

"I knew Horace several years ago. And, before you ask, yes, Gunderson before that. And Ford and Custer and Quicksilver before that." He paused. And I didn't want to upset him. So, I didn't press for more. "I told you, Rosa, that as you begin to understand Cyrandor, you'll see less of me. And, as it happens, so will I."

"Do you miss them?" I asked. "Horace and Gunderson and Quicksilver?" I liked that name. But August didn't have any silver any him that I could see. Perhaps he did then?

"I don't," he responded. "But I miss your Uncle and your

cousin. They're my family too."

"Are you glad I got lost? So, you could see them again?"

"I am glad you are safe, Rosa. And let's leave it at that, shall we?"

***

So, we did. "I go back to school tomorrow," I said, complying with his request. He asked if I liked my first day. Before the rain anyway. And, come to think of it, I liked all of it, in fact. Including the rain. And I told him so.

August laughed with pleasure at my revelation. "Yessir. That's my girl," he said between snickers. And he had an idea. Apparently, Mr. Dixon had something of a sweet tooth. So, August took me back to the tree I had found in the rain. The one with the candy apples on it. I picked one for my teacher, and one for my Uncle. And one for me and August. He told me not to pick too many because there weren't very many left on the tree. But I snuck one more. And I wouldn't tell him who it was for. In fact, I had hoped he didn't see me take it in the first place. Because I didn't know how to explain myself if he knew. I just stuffed it in my pocket. And did my best to puff out my clothing, so the bulge wouldn't show.

On the way back, August's gait was a bit slower. And we were both happy. He asked me to take it easy on Jasper. Not to hold a grudge against him. Because Jasper was really doing the right thing. He was minding his little brother. And seeing he got home safely. And, when he realized he forgot me, he went straight to Uncle Cheech.

I remembered that Jasper didn't think very much of August when we met. And I wondered how he felt about Gunderson. But I had agreed to leave the topic alone for a while. So, I didn't ask. But I thought I might ask Jasper at school tomorrow. Perhaps, at recess. Over a candy apple.

***

I said goodbye to August until, probably, the weekend. I was excited to go back to school. And I had a newfound confidence. I didn't fear the rain. I hoped to never be stranded in it again, but I knew I would be alright. And I felt as though I had friends in Cyrandor. And I had family in Cyrandor. And I trusted Mr. Dixon. And I trusted Cyrandor.

I walked back to the cottage with some leisure in my step. As I did I noted every tree, hillside, stream, pathway, and critter along the way. I had learned the importance of these things. And I was working on my awareness of my surroundings. This was the first task of my spy training. It wasn't about Jasper. I believe Jasper was part of the training. His abandonment during the rain must have been intentional. And, whether he knew why or not, he had been recruited to abandon me for this first important training mission. To learn to observe my surroundings. And so, I would.

And so, I did.

CHAPTER SEVENTEEN

I dreamt all night of August. And the rain. And Jasper. I don't dare believe my dreams. They whispered to me of hope. But also, of fear. And of tragedy. Mother always told me when I dreamed of terrible things that they were not to come to pass. But that I felt uncertain of something.

Or I ate something uncertain. Either way, I tried not to think too hard of my dream when I awoke. For another day presented itself. And a new day for school.

Jasper walked with me again. But we didn't say much on the journey. I took my place in the desk Mr. Dixon had assigned me on the first day. I continued to keep an eye on Jasper. Even though I knew. Even though I knew it wasn't necessary. But I did all the same.

And, somewhere in the midst of the day, I made a new friend. Or someone I hoped would be a friend. And nevertheless, she was. And her name was Titus.

I thought so too. It was a peculiar name for a girl. But she was nice. And funny. She was a year older than me, but that didn't matter. That didn't stop her from asking me to play at recess. And instead of Jasper, I shared my second candy apple with Titus. But I felt guilty all the same. And wished I had one more to share with Jasper. But I hadn't. And I didn't.

***

Titus had convinced Mr. Dixon to let her move desks, so she could be next to mine. Mr. Dixon liked Titus. She never raised any fuss. I didn't really either, apart from the other kids' curiosity. They had heard about me in the rain. They kept looking at me funny. Some of them liked to tease me about it. I didn't pay much mind to them. Papa always told me to ignore it when boys teased me. He said it's because they thought I was pretty. I used to think that was kind of gross. Now it makes me stand a little taller.

But most of the kids were nice to me about it – if they said anything at all. Usually they would encourage me, telling me I would figure it out. It wouldn't be long.

But it felt long already.

Titus reached over and picked up my pencil and pointed to something in my book with it. Then she set the pencil down and went back to her own book. Next to my pencil was now also a folded-up piece of paper. I didn't pick it up. I looked up at Mr. Dixon. He was facing the chalkboard. I looked over at Titus. She snickered and buried her nose in her book. I opened it up, but I could feel eyes on me. I looked again at Mr. Dixon. Still no. Then Titus. She continued to smile with her nose in her book.

But Jasper. I glanced his way and he quickly returned his eyes to his book as he blushed. I looked back at the paper in my hands. I accidentally smiled.

***

As it turns out Titus had terrible spelling. And pretty lousy handwriting. But I'm sure she was writing quickly, so I overlooked these shortcomings.

And when Mr. Dixon turned back to the chalkboard I picked up my pencil. I never thought Jasper had paid much attention to me. Especially knowing he had abandoned me in the rain and had little to say to me on our walk to school this morning. Yes, perhaps he was watching me a moment ago, but Titus implied that he never stops. I knew she was wrong. And though I smiled at the thought, I set her right. I wrote it in all capital letters.

HE IS NOT

And I giggled her direction, so she would know I wasn't angry at the thought. Quite the opposite, in fact. But Titus was too new a friend to confide so much. I hadn't really even confided so much to myself. And before I got ahead of myself, I very plainly wrote the name Hudson encircled with a heart on a different piece of paper. Because he was certainly more handsome. More so than Jasper. But with just the right smile, Jasper could--

Again, I stopped, put down my pencil, and began to refold the tiny piece of paper. I looked around me to be sure it was clear. And thrust the note back onto Titus' desk. She smirked and stopped it from sliding off the opposite side. Jasper looked again our direction. But not Mr. Dixon. He was still explaining the parameters of our first book report of the year. His back to the class and his hand at the chalkboard.

***

Titus read my response and rolled her eyes at me with a smile. I tried not to laugh and turned my attention to Mr. Dixon who had now turned back to address the class. "Please see me regarding your selection this afternoon. Dinna be a-waitin' for the last minute, yeh knaw," he advised.

I tried to focus again on Mr. Dixon. And Titus did too. I can't be certain of Jasper because I was afraid to look at him. But peripherally I could tell he was still at his desk. I began to take notes on the report. Mr. Dixon told us to copy the notes on the board. But while I wrote, my mind wandered. It was up to us to select a book, and I knew very few books to choose from.

I glanced at the bookshelf under the windows. There were a few kids already who knelt beside it looking for a suitable topic. I turned back to Titus who was still writing. And Jasper, who was simply staring off seemingly at nothing.

The younger ones didn't have to choose a book just yet. Tony was scratching out Math problems and some of the other kids were writing spelling words. Mr. Dixon looked my way and smiled. I smiled back and turned back to my notes. A moment later he was next to me.

"Di-ya have a book to choose from, Miss Rosa?" And I thought I probably did among some of Myra's books at the cottage. And I told Mr. Dixon so. "Ye'll let me know if ya need to borrow somethin'."

"Yes, sir," I responded. It was more formal than I was accustomed to being with Mr. Dixon, but we were in the classroom. Not by the creek or in Uncle's tool shed. I thought it best to use terms like "sir" around the other kids. He gave me another smile and a wink to let me know he would help in any way he could. I smiled again and continued writing my notes.

***

While Mr. Dixon and I spoke, Jasper had moved over to the bookshelf. As he sat on his knees examining the titles on each spine I noticed one that had a familiar look to it. It wasn't a bad idea. But I thought perhaps I should think about it a little more before making the decision.

This was my first real assignment for Mr. Dixon, you know. I didn't want to disappoint him. It was just the sort of question I could ask August. Which book is the right one? But August would think I was looking for the book to mean something. To be important. To have some kind of secret message in it. But it wouldn't have to. I just want Mr. Dixon to be proud of my work. And if the book happened to also shed some kind of spy light on the mysteries of Cyrandor, it wouldn't be a complete loss.

But again, that's what August would think I was after. So, I'd have to look for a book without a message. So that August wouldn't think I was so silly.

And without a love story too. Because I didn't need anyone else thinking I was silly either.

***

Again, I looked over at the bookshelf and focused in on the familiar spine. Jasper was still looking through the titles as well. I didn't want to, but I stood and walked over to it. Jasper saw me coming and I could feel Titus' eyes drawn to us. But I didn't speak to Jasper. I simply reached for the book and began to open it. I was still standing. I didn't dare kneel next to him.

I had barely flipped open the cover before Mr. Dixon called us all back to our seats. It was his custom, apparently, to dismiss us with a poem and a prayer. We hurried back, put our books and pencils away and stood at the sides of our desks.

I started on the left side of my desk, but Titus motioned me around to the other side. We were all to be on the right. One hand at our side, the other resting on the back of our chair. Facing forward with our heads up for the poem, and bowed for the prayer.

"Take thee, Wind, and lead us straight
Mind thee, Rain, our blessed fate
If fate be found, then quick thy gait
And be not lost nor be not late."

And then he prayed, and we started home. Titus joined us for the first stretch and left me and Jasper and Tony for the remainder.

***

Uncle Cheech greeted us at the front door with cookies. I gave him a sideways smile. He had never done that before. But he said that Grandpa always had cookies ready on the first day of school. That was a tradition that Uncle and my mother enjoyed growing up. Today wasn't the first day. But the first day got rained out. So, he prepared cookies for the second day. And shared one with Jasper and Tony too. They ate theirs as they continued on home. I bit into mine right away before I made it into the cottage and I managed to give a half-hearted goodbye to the Suttons before the cottage door closed behind me. And when Uncle and I sat down he couldn't wait to hear about school today.

I told him about Titus. And our book report. I told him I hadn't selected a book yet. Even though I thought about that one on the bookshelf. I told him that my favorite subject was Math. And that Titus moved her desk next to mine.

I liked school in Cyrandor. It wasn't all that different from school back home. But I liked it. In both places. And I looked forward to returning tomorrow. But I also missed seeing August. I had an idea that perhaps August could take me to school someday. Instead of Jasper. And I almost asked it of Uncle Cheech. But I didn't. I'm not sure why I didn't. But I didn't nonetheless.

***

As I headed to bed I plucked out the book with the familiar spine from the stack of books next to my cot. As I opened it I thought of Myra and imagined her there on the floor recounting her childhood in this very room.

I thought of Mother and Father and the way they used to take turns reading me to sleep each night. It wasn't intentional. And if I did fall asleep during the story they would always wake me to say my prayers. I missed those moments. And I knew I should have climbed out of bed to say my prayers at the memory. But I didn't. I don't know why I didn't. I thought of a few things I wanted to thank God for. And I submitted my thoughts heavenward. But I didn't climb out of bed. Instead I cracked open the book along with Father's timepiece which still hung around my neck. I laid down on my side and imagined Mother and Father were reading it to me.

And very shortly, I was asleep.

CHAPTER EIGHTEEN

I ate breakfast in a hurry because I knew I was running behind. I stepped out onto the porch and noticed the briskness of the air. I turned to go back inside and retrieve a sweater but, instead, caught sight of Jasper and Tony. Noticing I had already exited the cottage, Jasper gestured for me to catch up.

I clasped my arms as tightly as I could to keep warm on this cooler morning and ran to meet them.

"Where's your sweater, Rosa?" Jasper asked in a way that made me feel foolish. I hadn't experienced this cooler weather in Cyrandor before and Uncle mustn't have known to expect it because he didn't warn me about it. Nevertheless, it was a welcome change. And I wished I'd had my sweater to enjoy it more.

I had heard of chivalry and thought for a moment what I might do if Jasper had gone so far as to offer me his for the walk to school. But I had known at once my imagination had run away with me. He, of course, never offered and instead belittled me for my lack of warmer clothing.

It was unimportant. Had he offered, I would have refused, for certain. I could never fathom wearing something that belonged to such an inconsiderate dope. And the thought of arriving to school in such a garment was just as mortifying. If not more so. For what would Titus have to say?

***

Instead, Tony offered. I giggled. Jasper smacked his arm the way an older brother would. And we continued on to school. I with my arms wrapped tightly together and Tony with my books. Jasper sped ahead of us a bit. Again, I smiled.

The cooler air had a different smell. It reminded me of home. I thought about the evenings we spent outside by the fire and wondered if they had similar traditions in Cyrandor. Or if the leaves changed colors like they do back home.

As we neared the schoolhouse, I could hear someone calling my name. I turned around to see Uncle Cheech in his work clothes holding out my sweater. Or, rather, Myra's sweater. Nevertheless, it was mine all the same. And Uncle was the chivalrous one. I ran back to him to retrieve it and he kissed the top of my head like all the grown-ups in my family seemed accustomed to do. I gave him a quick hug and rejoined my friends.

Or Jasper and Tony anyway.

***

As I was sliding into my desk for the morning Mr. Dixon rang the bell and we all stood for the morning prayer. Again, on the right with my left hand on the back of the chair. My head was bowed, but I kept one eye open. I assumed God knew my family business. So, I thought it was okay to keep one open during prayer.

After the "amen" we all sat down and started the day. It passed the same as yesterday. Math, History, Science, Lunch, Recess, Grammar, and Literature. With some time at the end to work on our book reports.

After school we made our way back home, and Cheech and I had dinner, the usual "how-was-your-day" conversation, and another quiet evening before turning in.

This was how the days passed for the remainder of the week. On Saturday, I went to see August. And I told him all about school. And Titus. And how Titus thought Jasper paid lots of attention to me. And I told him about Math class, and the book report. I told him about the book I was going to use, but I didn't make a fuss over it. His only response was to wonder if I had started reading it yet. And, of course, I had. At least that first night I had. But not since. And it was probably a good idea to get a jump on it. August was always right about those kinds of things.

I asked August how cold it gets in Cyrandor. Because it was pretty cold, one morning, this week. And I wondered if August ever needed an extra coat. But he stayed warm enough, he said. And for a while, this will be as cold as it gets. But when it gets on toward Christmas, Cyrandor has seen snow a time or two. But only a time or two. Not every Christmas.

***

August and I sat quietly for a bit, enjoying the afternoon. It was the first time we had seen each other since school began. Or, at least, since it began again. He was a very wise horse. And even though I thought of him as my very best friend in Cyrandor, he was also much older. And I was often eager for his advice. Today it wasn't necessarily advice I was after, but I did wonder. I wondered about Jasper. I thought I was probably too young to wonder too much about boys. And yet I wondered if Jasper really did pay much attention to me. And if so, was there a reason for it? A reason other than the reason I sometimes secretly hoped for.

"Do you think--" I began. But I stopped. And August didn't press for more. It's as if he knew what I was thinking. And he continued to graze in the clearing, neither acknowledging that I spoke, nor that I had stopped.

I reconsidered the question. But I began again. "Do you think Titus is right?" Again, August continued to graze. Remaining silent at the thought. I felt a little foolish. I hopped down from my perch and went over next to him. I sat down right in the grass next to his head and looked him square in the eye. "Do you?" I asked one more time. This time he snickered.

"Climb on," he said, throwing his head back a bit to motion me onto his back. "There's more to it than that. But the short of it is, yes. Titus is right." I smiled at the thought and then was struck with the disappointment that perhaps August and I were not talking about the same thing.

"I mean about Jasper," I clarified.

"So do I," whispered August.

***

"Does that mean--"

"Now, Rosa," he interrupted. "You know I can't go telling you everything, now can I?" And he couldn't. What kind of spy would I be just listening to my talking horse friend. But I did listen all the same. "You know how mysterious Cyrandor is, right? How you're always trying to figure it out? Well that's how Jasper feels. About you."

"How do you know that?" But I knew he was right. Even though it made me feel kind of sorry for Jasper. But August just knows things. He's been in Cyrandor a long time. And he's been many different horses.

"But there's a lot more to it than that." And I waited for him to go on, but he didn't. All the same it made me feel sort of different about Jasper. And sort of the same.

***

I watched the rainbows drift by as August and I rode home that afternoon. There were a great many for a Saturday. I wondered if it was all the same rainbow that I watched. And it moved with the landscape as we journeyed. I wished I could understand the landscape. But if my choice was between knowing August or the landscape, I much preferred August.

I leaned into his neck and held on. He knew what I meant by it, and he took off, going faster and faster. So fast that I nearly slid off, but he jerked in such a way to help me regain my balance. Never losing speed. I imagined all those rainbows standing right above us as we raced under each one. In my imagination, they glowed brighter each time we cleared one.

The wind blew my long, tangled hair behind me, and I could feel the cool breezes on my face and neck. It was even a cooler breeze than before. I spotted a few Heckella Bushes as we raced past. And the familiar candy apple tree. I even glimpsed the creek a few times, and for a moment, Uncle's tool shed.

And before I knew it, August was slowing to a trot. And I saw Uncle's cottage ahead. He already had a fire going. And the aroma of dinner. But not the kind of dinner for just me and

Uncle Cheech. I could tell it was special. And I hoped it was Myra. And Hudson, of course.

***

"Uncle Cheech?" I shouted as I came through the cottage door. But Uncle wasn't there. And neither was Myra. Or Hudson. It felt eerie. And I became scared, backing to the wall, hoping to remain in the shadows.

I saw the shadow of somebody around the corner in the kitchen. And I slid quietly toward the fireplace, looking for a poker for defense. As the shadow moved, the fear again rose inside me. And my spy instincts failed me. Not entirely, for I knew he was coming closer. I knew he was about to enter the room. But I lost all courage. I screamed as he entered. I dropped the poker back into the fireplace and raced for the door.

I could feel him coming after me, but I ran from the porch toward the wall where I knew I'd meet August. I ran as fast as I could. All the while wiping the hair from my face. And the tears, and sweat.

And then I stopped. Even though he was fast approaching. I stopped. I stopped because I wasn't afraid anymore. I stopped. Not because my side hurt. But it did. I stopped because--

***

"Rosa!" called Grandpa to me from behind.

I stopped because I had recognized the shadow. And I cried from the fear. And from the relief. And from the happiness of seeing Grandpa. I cried. I sat down right in the road. In the gravel. Between the cottage and the stone wall. And Grandpa sat with me.

Grandpas always have handkerchiefs, I think. And he did. And rather than offering it to me, he did the Grandpa kind of thing. He held it in his own hands and wiped my eyes and my face as I leaned into his chest. Huddled in his arms.

I love Uncle Cheech. And I was beginning to love Cyrandor. But I missed Grandpa. And I missed home. And I cried. For a good long time. And then Grandpa helped me up, took my hand, and walked me back to the cottage.

"It's going to be alright, Rosa," he said in that comforting gravelly voice he had. And I knew it would be. Grandpa was here. And everything was going to be alright.

**

He held my hand as we walked back to the cottage. The other hand stuffed the handkerchief back in his pocket and pointed at the fountain, commenting on the rainbows in the spray of the water. I admired it, remembering that apart from Uncle's cottage, it was the first thing I had seen in Cyrandor. Just after Grandpa dropped me off.

We had roast beef and mashed potatoes for dinner. Grandpa fixed it all. I could even taste the Heckella Root. I even bet it was Grandpa that taught Myra how to cook. Or it could have been Aunt Kelly. Nevertheless, Grandpa's food was delicious. I wished Uncle Cheech could have been there to enjoy it with us.

Grandpa had told me that Uncle Cheech was going to be late getting home. So, he made sure I was fed and looked after. But I knew better. Uncle had put me up to a new spy challenge.

And Grandpa was in on it. I only had to turn the conversation a little to discover what it was.

"Why don't you live in Cyrandor, anymore, Grandpa?" I asked. Surely, it was spy-related. But he said he wanted to be closer to me after Myra grew up. That was nice of him. But now I was in Cyrandor. "Will you ever move back?" I asked again. But he didn't know. He told me that you can't always predict life as it sits before you. You can't plan out circumstances and know how you'd behave in those moments. But he was happy to be visiting me tonight. And that we'd discuss it more in the morning.

And I would see to it that we would. And we most certainly did.

CHAPTER NINETEEN

I awoke excited to have Grandpa and Uncle Cheech together with me at church this morning. I got dressed and combed my hair quickly. I grabbed my Bible from the trunk next to my cot. I had actually opened and read it last night with the excitement of Grandpa being there. As I left my room and came around the corner to the kitchen, there was still no sign of Uncle. No lingering smell of his cigarette from the night before. No trace of his typical scrambled eggs and toast.

Grandpa had breakfast ready, but the table was only set for the two of us. And I wondered exactly how late Uncle was going to be. But I didn't ask. I didn't even ask Grandpa about moving back to Cyrandor. I ate my breakfast in silence, while Grandpa read a passage from the Bible.

That was how Grandpa did mornings. Bacon and eggs and sausage. And the Bible. Most of the time, my mind drifted while Grandpa read. At home, Mother and Father would shush me if I tried to speak during that time. So, I sat quietly. I didn't pay close attention, but occasionally I would catch a "thither" or "thou". I felt bad because he didn't get much of a chance to eat his breakfast between thithers. I wanted to offer to read a little for him, so he could eat. But I wasn't supposed to speak. So, I didn't. And Grandpa continued.

***

Mr. Sutton was preaching this morning, because Mr. Blake was out of town. I wondered if Mr. Blake and Uncle Cheech were together. And my spy senses kicked in. They had to be together. That was it! But why? I looked around for Jasper because he always seems to be connected with these things. But he was sitting in the front with his mother and Tony and Lila. Titus' family had come in late and were able to slide into the pew next to me and Grandpa.

Grandpa, incidentally sits in the back. Not the very back row, but the back, nonetheless. I imagine if Uncle were with us, we'd have sat a little closer. But maybe not. Because Grandpa was Uncle's father. And so, he would have the final say. Nevertheless, there we were with Titus' family. In the back. Titus and I knew not to giggle and talk during the sermon, so we sat nicely and listened. Well, we sat nicely, anyway.

With Uncle, I knew I had to listen enough to discuss the sermon after church, because Uncle always liked to talk about what Mr. Blake or Mr. Sutton had to say. Then Uncle would sort of say it again in a new way. A way he thought I could understand better. And a little bit shorter than the sermon. But only a little bit.

But Uncle wasn't here today, so I didn't have to pay as close attention. So, I tried my very best to determine why he wasn't there. And why wasn't Mr. Blake? And then suddenly it hit me!

Uncle is a groundskeeper! Mr. Blake is a preacher! Where would you find the two of them together? At a graveyard! So, the next question was, who died? And I began to scan the congregation to see if I could determine who else was missing...

***

I scanned each row, left to right, right to left, front to back. I scanned the choir seats and the two rows behind us. I thought about each of my classmates and they were all accounted for. I thought about Mr. Dixon, and Myra and Hudson. But, of

course, Myra and Hudson weren't there. I looked beside me to be certain Grandpa and Titus' family hadn't disappeared. Everyone was there.
Next, I began to count, and I checked the board on the wall to see how many were in attendance last week. This week we were down one person. I was right! Someone had died! I began to panic. As much as a spy listening nicely to a sermon could panic, anyway. I went through each family again. Checking for both parents, if necessary, and any children. I tapped at my forehead to think about anybody I was missing. Anybody I was forgetting about. Knowing full well, that I didn't know everybody in Cyrandor. Or everybody at church. Titus gave me a sideways glance when I did that. I gave a quick scratch to my temple as though I had just swatted away a fly. Which I hadn't. But I didn't want to look suspicious.

In my despair, I devised another plan. Immediately after the service I'd go find August. And we'd go directly to the graveyard. And the thought gave me a chill. So, I devised a new plan.

Immediately after the service, I'd go find Jasper. And we'd go find August. And we'd go directly to the graveyard.

***

I waited on the steps for Grandpa. People hadn't seen him in a while, so he was very popular after the service. Lots of hugs and handshakes. And pats on the back. I was impatient. But I waited. Titus and I played with the spinner she brought in her dress pocket, and I kept a close eye on Jasper so as to catch him before he left.

When Titus left with her family, I found myself even more impatient. I slipped over near Jasper, and tried to gesture him over. He raised both eyebrows as I motioned more energetically. He wasn't very bright. I gave one final gesture and then glanced over to see where Grandpa was.

I hadn't figured out how to tell Grandpa where I was going, but I had to be sure I had a security team with me. By the time I looked back at Jasper, he had disappeared.

"What's all this about Rosie?" I heard whispered from behind me. The surprise of it made me jump. I started to tell him, but felt too suspicious out in the open. I grabbed his hand and hurried to the side of the building. "Rosa!" he shouted, following me, and tripping along the way. I turned and shushed him to keep our cover.

"You have to come with me this afternoon," I told him. But he still looked confused. "With August!" I clarified. Again, there was silence. "Look, Uncle Cheech didn't come home last night. And now, Mr. Blake is gone--"

"Aw, I know about that. Pops kicks in when he's out of town. I told you that," he submitted. I rolled my eyes. He wasn't getting it.

I tried to explain a little better. And I enunciated, "CheECH and Mr. BlaKE are BOTH gone!" I'm pretty sure Jasper thought I was the dumb one. But I needed someone to go with me to the graveyard. And I don't think Grandpa would have supported the notion. Titus wouldn't have offered any protection. It HAD to be Jasper. "Nevermind. Listen. You have to go with me to find August."

***

"Again, with the horse," he responded. I could feel my expression sink. I knew every part of my non-spy exterior betrayed my confident facade. He glanced over my shoulder at his family, clumped in conversation with my Grandpa. "Look, Rosa. I don't know what this is all about, but--" he stopped. He had kind of a new brightness in his face. And a smirk slid across his face. And a dimple appeared. He looked at me in silence for a minute. I merely waited for him to go on. I didn't notice the silence until he finally did go on.

"I'll figure something out. I'll come by the cottage in an hour or so," and he stuck out his hand as if we were shaking on a deal. I took it. And followed him back to the circle of Suttons. And Grandpa.

The nice thing about Grandpas is that they take naps in the afternoon. And my Grandpa was as Grandpa as you can get in that regard. So, there wasn't any story to make up. Or excuse to conjure. I simply waited for him to drift off, and went out on the porch to wait for Jasper.

It was pretty close to an hour, just like he said. And there he came, with that ridiculous twig hanging out of his mouth. I didn't wait for him to get to the porch. I leapt off and ran to him, grabbing his hand and pulling him back the other way, toward August. Again, he followed for a moment and then stopped, but never letting go of me. In fact, he stopped so quickly it jerked me back around.

"Rosa, you've got to tell me what we're doing!"

* * *

So, I began.

"Uncle Cheech didn't come home last night," I started.

Again, he interrupted "I know that, Rosa. And Mr. Blake--" I slapped my hand over his mouth in an unintentionally forceful way.

"I know you think you understand. But let me tell you what's happening. And stop interrupting me." He nodded. Still with my hand over his mouth. Finally, I released him. "Uncle Cheech is still not home. And Mr. Blake is not here either." I then explained the part about the Groundskeeper and the Preacher and the graveyard, and how we were short one person at church today, and that I had to take August to the graveyard, but that I couldn't go alone, and that he had to come with me.

And a little bit how I didn't know where the graveyard was. And then I was done.

"Look, Rosa." And I knew he was going to disagree with me again. So, I involuntarily slapped my hand over his mouth once more. And suddenly he was agreeable again. It was nice knowing I had a newfound authority. As we started toward August, Jasper's protests began again. I wheeled around to once more silence him and he caught my wrist, twisting my arm in such a way to not quite hurt. But I knew it could if he pushed any harder. The silencing authority was over. "Rosa, listen to me!" he asserted.

So, I did.

***

"August can't take you to the graveyard." I didn't know if it was the truth or not. But I listened to him. He didn't believe in what I was saying. But he said he'd take me. But August couldn't. I wanted to know for sure. I wanted to race down the path to August and find out why. But I wanted to believe Jasper. I wanted to trust him. And I didn't want to hurt August. If there was a reason he couldn't go, I'd rather not bring it up at all.

But I'd feel better, all the same if he were with me. And I had second thoughts of going at all. What if Jasper was right? What if nobody was hurt? Maybe there were other places to look first. Maybe my instincts were all wrong. And that Uncle Cheech was just "out" and would be back "late".

But what if I wasn't wrong? I had to know. I had to know for myself. And Jasper was my friend. He was willing to go with me, even though he thought I was wrong.

(Although, maybe he wanted to be there to laugh at me when I found he was right).

***

It wasn't a long walk, but it was different. It felt different than Cyrandor had felt before. Even different than when it rains. It didn't look familiar. And though I didn't mean to, I found myself holding onto Jasper the further we walked. And I think I even held on tighter.

For a while the gravel road led into a stone path. It was still sunny. It wasn't dark and mysterious the way you'd think a graveyard would be. It was bright. And well kept. There was a stone wall, like much of Cyrandor had, surrounding it. The entrance too was made up of stone pillars connected by an arc at the top.

We stopped before going in. You could see clear in to the back of the yard, over the wall or through the gate. There was clearly nobody there, apart from the grave markers of Cyrandor's ancestors. I was frightened of it all the same. I didn't believe I was wrong. But I had no proof I was right without passing through the archway. Still I couldn't make my feet move.

The truth is, I didn't want to be right. I wanted to be wrong. I wanted to know that everyone in Cyrandor was safe. Including Uncle Cheech. And Mr. Blake. And whoever else was missing from church.

The smaller part of me that wanted to be right couldn't convince myself to prove it. I couldn't go. Jasper and I stood and stared at the entrance. And then turned back the way we came. And back to the cottage. Not knowing the result. And neither solving the mystery of Uncle Cheech and Mr. Blake.

But Jasper didn't laugh. He just held my hand as we walked the short distance home.

***

Grandpa was still asleep when we got back. Jasper went on home and I tiptoed back inside so as not to wake him. Uncle Cheech hadn't returned yet either. And I wondered still whether we should have passed on through the archway. Through to the graveyard. To search in hidden corners and crevices. Or look for freshly laid stones. I wasn't entirely disappointed in myself for not looking. And yet I was, too. Being a spy, you can't be afraid of things. Or maybe you can, but you have to be able to do them, even when you are afraid. And I couldn't. Even with Jasper. Even with him right there beside me.

Before I went to bed, I prayed for everyone I knew. I even prayed for everyone I didn't know. I prayed that everyone was home and safe with their families. I prayed for Uncle and Mr.

Blake too, even though I knew Uncle wasn't home. And I prayed for Mother and Father. Because I didn't know. But I prayed for them. And I prayed for Grandpa, too.

And then I laid on my cot waiting for the comforting aroma to waft around the corner of my room, so that I could fall asleep, knowing Uncle was home. But there never was. And he wasn't. But Grandpa was there. And I could hear him cough once or twice each time he stirred the logs of the fire. And later, I could hear him snore. And soon, I began to snore too. But not as loudly.

CHAPTER TWENTY

I finished giving my report and the class applauded. It seemed like they only did so because that's what they were supposed to do whenever someone presented in class. They chuckled kindly when I acted parts of it out. And some of them were nice enough not to laugh when Mr. Dixon corrected my pronunciation of the title. But even with all of that, I was proud of the work I had done. Proud that I hadn't missed school yet as Mr. Dixon had predicted. And proud that I had completed our first book report. And proud of the applause. Even though it was required.

Titus went after me and even used funny voices in her report. The kids really liked her. Mr. Dixon did too. I saw him wipe a tear from his eye after we all laughed at one of her voices. It was kind laughter. And Titus laughed too. That was her intent.

Titus was taller than me and had short hair that flipped out at the ends. She wore a pair of glasses with pink diamonds on the sides. She told me they weren't diamonds, but they may as well have been. They looked an awful lot like what I imagine diamonds look like. Nevertheless, they weren't. But I liked her glasses because of them. She'd let me try them on from time to time and everything got very blurry when I did. I couldn't imagine them helping anybody to see. But they worked for Titus. So, they must have been magical. And I guess they were. Because everything in Cyrandor seemed to be made of magic. I wondered sometimes if they made Titus funny too. Because she was really good at making people laugh.

So, when Titus finished her book report, not only did the class applaud like they were supposed to, but they cheered for her. We all wanted to read her book because of her report. We cheered, and she bowed. She didn't seem embarrassed by the attention. She just took a funny bow and kept us cheering until she made her way back to her seat.

***

Mr. Dixon sat down with me at lunchtime to talk about my book report. He told me he always does that sort of thing - meet with us at lunch. But it was the first time it happened to me. I offered to share my grapes with him, but he just chuckled and thanked me, nonetheless. He also offered me a few of his crackers that his wife had packed him. They tasted like pickles, but I ate them anyway.

He was proud of the book I had chosen. He said it was a perfect fit. I thought that was a good way to start my evaluation, and I started to smile, looking forward to the rest of his thoughts on it. He also liked that I acted out a scene from it. It was one more way that the book "suited me," as he put it. But my report was apparently not worthy of an A, just yet. He wanted me to redo my report. And he wanted me to ask Uncle Cheech to help me. He even thought I should spend another day with Uncle at his work, to help me out.

I was puzzled. I never knew a teacher to have me redo an assignment. If it wasn't an A, it was something else. But it wasn't an opportunity to do it over. Nevertheless, Mr. Dixon insisted.

One of the reasons I was proud of my report is that I didn't get help. From anyone. I went straight to the bookshelf. I chose the book. I read the book. I reported on the book. I presented my report. I was ready to accept my grade.

***

I liked Mr. Dixon. But I was growing frustrated. This was not how things are done. I did the assignment. I'm ready for the next. I'm not ready to spend my entire year -- well, what's left of my eight months anyway -- doing the same project over and over and over again. It was time for me to take a stand. It was time for me to tell Mr. Dixon what should be done.

I swallowed my grape and stood up. Slowly. And then I reached for one more pickle-cracker. Mr. Dixon watched me, waiting for what I was about to say. I waited too. It took an unusually long time to chew up the cracker. And I couldn't tell Mr. Dixon what I was feeling over a mouthful of cracker crumbs. And once I had finally swallowed, I needed more time. I took a drink to wash it all down.

Mr. Dixon continued to wait. I looked back at him a few seconds longer and then finally picked up my report from in front of him. I looked it over, with his grade markings. I noticed he had doodled a little gondolier smiling back at me at the bottom of the page. Again, I looked back at him and finally spoke.

"Yes, sir," I said.

***

Mr. Dixon smiled his soothing grin. He had tiny white whiskers that covered his chin and upper lip. His white hair was a bit tousled and not without added white from the chalk he always had in his hand. He pointed at my grapes as if to accept one after all. I nodded. He picked it up and popped it in the air before catching it in his mouth. Then he grinned, winked, and went over to talk to another student.

I looked again at the drawing on my report. It was similar to the one on the cover of the book, without the smile. Mr. Dixon was a great teacher, but not a very good artist. The figure's arms and legs were mere sticks, compared to the book's cover. And the hair on his head was just a few strands poking straight out the top.

I wanted the kids to like my book the way they liked Titus's just because of my report. So, I thought maybe it wasn't a bad idea to redo the report. Maybe I could even do a drawing, like Mr. Dixon had done. Only better. But whatever I did, it was going to be great. I'd even get an A. And the kids would want to read my book too. Maybe even Jasper would. At least I hoped he would.

I rushed back to the cottage. Uncle was supposed to finally be home today. I couldn't wait to tell him about my book report. And to ask to go back to work with him. And sure enough, he was. And I did.

***

Uncle didn't answer me about going to work with him. In fact, as soon as I asked, the familiar sound of rain hit the windows. And I knew he wouldn't be going anywhere until it passed. I was certain Myra and Hudson would be arriving in the morning. And their arrival would mean more games like Dozy Joker, and more cooking, and mud masks, and giggling into the wee hours of the night.

I liked it when Myra was here. And I couldn't wait for morning. But I wondered all the same whether Uncle would allow me to stay home when the rain had passed. And to go with him back to his shed. I didn't know whether I would learn anything about the book by going with him. But I'd have to include something from the experience. Because it seemed important to Mr. Dixon. So important he was willing to let me out of school for it. So, I hoped it was important to Uncle Cheech.

Cheech fixed ham and eggs for supper. Every now and then Mother would fix that for breakfast. But never for supper. Cheech on the other hand insisted that it didn't matter when in the day you ate the eggs, they still tasted the same. I thought they tasted a little different for dinner. But only because it was Uncle Cheech who made them. And not Mother. But I ate them anyway.

And as Uncle and I sat by the fire that evening and listened to the rain, he became unusually talkative. "Do you think Mr. Dixon will let you take a rain check on that book report?" he asked. I assumed Mr. Dixon wasn't planning for me to go out in the rain, so I was certain he would. But Uncle wasn't ready, even after the rain. He thought maybe in a week or two I could go with him again. But not quite yet. I was a little disappointed, but I told him that it would probably be okay. And Uncle asked what book I was reporting on.

I ran into my little room and pulled the book from the up-turned trunk. "This one," I said holding it out to my Uncle.

***

Uncle just stared at it blankly for a moment. Then he reached for it slowly, and held it down to view it in the firelight. He seemed fascinated by it. The way I hoped the other kids would react when I presented again on it. "You, uh," he started. And then he stopped. He reached in his shirt pocket and pulled out a pack of gum. As he offered me a piece, he took one for himself as well. "You chose this book?" he asked.

I nodded. He grunted and began to leaf through the pages. He smirked a bit. I assumed he was amused at the markings on the inside that were there before Myra even owned it. "You read this?" he asked again. I nodded again. And again, a grunt of satisfaction.

"Have you read it before?" I asked. Another grunt. "Did you like it?"

"I still do," he responded with bright eyes. "Come over here for a second." So, I did. I sat down right next to him as he thumbed through the pages, a wisp-ish expression on his face. "You see that?" he asked as he pointed to a paragraph in the middle.

I began to read, "As the sun rose higher in the sky, Calvin pushed in harder into the sea. He knew the strength of the oar in his hands and practiced every day to become more like --" Uncle stopped me and grinned. "Calvin?" I asked. "Like you!" He nodded with a smile.

"You see these markings? I did that. When I was just a child. Your mother did a few of them too." I giggled. And marveled at my Mother's childish scratchings. I pulled out the time piece that hung around my neck. Uncle sighed a happy sigh. "Let's have a look at that, shall we?" And we did.

***

He told me stories about Mother as a little girl. She had trouble pronouncing his name, so he became Cheech. And it just stuck. Though personally I think Calvin is easier than Cheech. But I'm not my Mother.

Mother loved to eat mashed potatoes, so for a while Grandma would serve her mashed potatoes for every meal. Grandpa and

Cheech would eat pancakes and sausages. And Mother and Grandma, mashed potatoes. And the funny thing is that Mother makes wonderful mashed potatoes now. They're my favorite meal too. And I liked that we had that in common.

I told Uncle that I missed my Mother and Father. And he did too. "When will I see them again," I wanted to ask. But questions like that usually meant that Uncle was done talking, and it was time for bed. So, I didn't ask. But I hugged Father's time piece tight that night as I slept. And I dreamt I was eating a whole plate full of mashed potatoes.

As I slept, I was comforted by the aroma wafting around the corner, as it had so often done since I had arrived in Cyrandor. I still wondered why it was absent the past couple of days. But it didn't matter as much as the fact that it had returned once again.

***

Sure enough, Myra and Hudson arrived in the morning. In fact, Myra already had breakfast sizzling before I even awoke. But I could smell it. And the smell opened my eyes. And I couldn't wait to get out to greet them. On this visit, it was in reality Hudson doing the standing and the cooking. But Myra was coaching from the kitchen table.

Hudson looked handsome (and a little funny) in the cooking apron. But the sparkle in his teeth still managed to evoke the sound of a bell when he smiled. I was happy to see them. I ran to greet them and was, as usual, kissed atop my head from both of them. But not at the same time.

"How's my favorite little cousin?" asked Myra as I sat down at the table, still in my nightgown. I told her about my book report, and that Grandpa came to stay for a while. But I didn't mention the graveyard. At least not yet. "Oh, how I miss our Grandpa!" she exclaimed.

"Haven't you seen him in a while?" I asked, knowing that Grandpa didn't live in Cyrandor anymore. I thought perhaps he lived close to Myra. And he did. But she still hadn't seen him in a few weeks. She said she misses Grandpa just like she misses me and Uncle Cheech when she's not here. I knew what she meant. I missed her too. And sometimes I even miss August when I'm in school. And Jasper, when it rains. But I didn't say so. I think Myra probably knew. But I didn't say so.

Myra was excited to hear that I had chosen "The Gondolier" for my book report. She told me again how it was her favorite. And how it reminded her of her father. I figured it's because it shared his name. And she thought so too. But somehow it was more than that. But probably it was mostly the name.

***

William's breakfast was awfully delicious. Even though it wasn't actually Myra who made it. But William had a way of making things seem better, too. And I don't even think it was Heckella Root. But rather just his way with things. Like his smile. And his hugs. They were good like his breakfast. I just wondered why he hadn't done better with his name. But I was coming around to William. It was still a strong name. A good name. But so was Hudson.

"Do you know Uncle made me breakfast for dinner last night?" I said.

"Oh my! Well we should have had steak and mushrooms this morning, then!" exclaimed William with a smirk. I laughed.

"You know, breakfast for dinner was the first meal I ever shared with Cheech and Myra," he went on. It was a school break and he came for dinner to get to know Uncle. But he said he already planned to propose to Myra. And while he needed Cheech's permission, he couldn't wait to meet and get to know the "gentle giant," as Myra called him.

It was funny. I had never thought of Uncle that way before, but that's certainly a good description of him. I guess you have to be pretty big and strong to do the kind of grounds work that he is tasked with. Come to think of it, it's probably helpful in spyhood, too. That's why Father is so strong. I remember a few years ago that I used to hang onto just his arm and he would raise me way up off the ground as we walked. Plucking me up over puddles and stones and anything else in our way. He lifted me up as though I weighed nothing at all. Perhaps all fathers are strong.

But not as strong as the ones in my family. And William probably is too. But I've never seen him demonstrate it.

***

Uncle still hadn't joined us, and with a mouth full of eggs I began to think about Grandpa again. And why he had come. And where Uncle had gone. And Mr. Blake. And the graveyard.

"Should I have gone in?" I asked aloud. And through a few unchewed bits of egg. Myra and William looked at me quizzically. William cocked his head. I had forgotten to express the rest of my thoughts aloud. Only the final question. And then I wondered whether I ought to express the rest. Or even that final question. And there was silence as Myra and William waited for me to go on. And I pondered how to rephrase the question in a way that had something to do with the current moment. And less to do with a graveyard. The silence grew quite loud, the longer it lasted. And finally, William broke it.

"Sorry, Rosa. I must have gotten caught up in thought. Where is it you were going?"

I really wanted to go on. I wanted to go ahead and tell them all about the graveyard. And at the same time, I didn't. I wanted to think of something. Anything. I wanted to keep from seeming so absurd. And the silence again became overwhelming.

"Rosa?" Myra queried. And then she laughed. "Rosa, you are a funny girl! I think you must have gotten a bit caught up yourself," she giggled. And so did I. I laughed because it was fun. I laughed because Myra was laughing. And so had William started to. And I laughed because it seemed to be a good way to not repeat the question. Or explain the question. And I laughed because the thought of Uncle hiding in a tiny corner of the graveyard with Mr. Blake, out of plain sight seemed suddenly absurd.

But still I wondered all the same.

***

In the laughter I remembered to tell them about Titus, because Titus would have laughed too if she were there. Uncle joined us some time in the midst of my stories about Titus and how she thought Jasper thought a lot about me. But August said it was because he doesn't understand me. Like I don't understand Cyrandor.

When I brought that part up, though the three of them seemed to exchange glances. As if they were trying to do so secretly.

But I saw. I didn't say that I saw. But I saw. And then Uncle began to talk about the time the Suttons came for dinner.

"Did you know the Suttons married of their own will?" he asked. Apparently to Myra and William, because I did. I saw Hudson smile and his arm shifted under the table toward Myra. I assumed he was holding her hand. Myra smiled his direction. And raised an eyebrow at Uncle. She didn't remember that about the Suttons. "Sure enough. Made their own plans regarding the whole event. Interesting now, isn't it?" I still didn't find that all that interesting. I found it interesting that Cyrandor made such a habit of making the decision for people. That was the odd choice. Not deciding for yourself. When it comes time for me to decide, I imagine it will be someone like Hudson. Or Jas---

I coughed and sputtered for a moment. I couldn't believe it had come to this. That smelly old darthead was stuck in my head. I actually not only tolerated him, I liked him. And not just that, but I pictured myself with him. I--

I--

It's not possible. I like him?

I LIKE him. I like him. A LOT. This has to be unreal.

***

But the unreal part was yet to come. And if I had known, I would have left the breakfast table long beforehand. I should have read their faces. Their looks. Their glances. The raised eyebrows. The holding hands. I should have known it. I should have read it. That's my JOB.

I'M. A. SPY.

I should have seen where this was going. But I didn't. I missed it. And when it hit, I couldn't help the way I responded. It. Was. Un. Real.

"Rosa," And the silence between my name and the rest of it was long and painful. It was as if they knew it was wrong. Like they knew it was unreal too. But unfortunately, they didn't. They ended the silence. And went on. Or rather Uncle went on. And the others watched. In silence and calm.

"You are betrothed."

CHAPTER TWENTY-ONE

It had been hours since I left my room. They couldn't have expected me to come out. Not after such an announcement. I didn't move. I didn't lay down. I didn't stand up. I didn't pace. I didn't focus on anything. But I stared at the wall, from the edge of my cot. I stared wondering how they could have made the decision for me. I didn't want to get married. And certainly not until I'm older. And I know that the wedding wasn't right away. But now it existed. And it hadn't before. And until this very morning, my only feeling in the world was excitement to see my cousin. And her husband. But now I hated husbands. Not William of course, but the idea of them. It was not in my plan. And I hated that there even was a plan.

So, I sat on the edge of my cot and stared at the wall. The age of the cottage was apparent in its color. The floors squeaked outside my room, but I ignored them. I ignored all of them. And suddenly, Cyrandor had lost all of its magic. I simply wanted to go home. I began to plan. Not for husbands and weddings, but to leave. To go back home. To Mother and Father. And sometimes Grandpa. I planned to leave at night. When the familiar aroma wafts away as Uncle slips into sleep in the chair. I planned what I would pack. I wondered whether to see August before I left. I wondered whether he would help me get back home. I planned how to ask him. And not to ask Jasper. I wasn't sure about Titus. I didn't know whether to bring her with me. But she probably knew all along about the betrothal. And a friend would have said something. So, I should probably leave her out of the plan as well.

So, there was August. And Mr. Dixon. And Mr. Blake. They had not betrayed me. Neither had Jasper, really. But I couldn't go to him. Because maybe he knew, too. And maybe Mr. Blake

knew after all. Maybe that's why he and Uncle were away.
Maybe they were planning my betrothal. But to whom?
None of that mattered anymore. I was not going to marry.
Anyone. I was going home. And that was all there was to it.

***

And if I was going to leave, then this could be the last day I
spent with Uncle and Myra. And no matter how angry I felt, I
still loved them. So, I chose to stand up. To stop staring. To
focus on something other than weddings and escapes. So, I
chose to stand up. And I left my cot and my room. And I
rejoined the group in the other room.

I wanted to sneak out and casually merge back into their
company. But I knew they were all aware I was back from the
moment I rejoined them. It didn't matter. As long as they didn't
talk about betrothal. And they didn't. Which was nice.

I rejoined them silently. I didn't say much. And they didn't
insist that I did. They just continued on as if nothing had
happened. And it angered me. But I was grateful for it. I
wanted it to matter. Not so much "it" but "me." I wanted to
matter. But I didn't want to acknowledge it. So, the confusion
of wanting acknowledgement and anonymity at the same time
was something I wasn't used to.

They had suggested a game of cards. And I wasn't interested.
But in order to not play I would have had to raise my voice and
demand it. So, I kept quiet and joined in. I hated it. Every
moment. And inside knowing that it might be the last evening I
ever spent in their company -- or at least for a very long time --
I loved it. I captured every moment with a fake smile.
Pretending I was over it. Or that it hadn't happened. Or that I
wasn't leaving. Pretending, for a very short time, that I was in

charge. And could make my own decisions. Because, apparently, I couldn't.

***

Soon, I had drifted off to sleep. I didn't mean to. And I certainly didn't want to fall asleep on Uncle Cheech. But I did. I was curled up underneath his arm and fell right to sleep.

I don't remember Uncle trying to send me back to my room. I don't remember the smell of his cigarette. I just remember that I slept deeply. As though I meant it. And I didn't. But I did.

I do remember dreaming that there was something important that needed to be done. And that I just couldn't lift my arms to do whatever it was. It felt as though they were pulled to my side by some unforeseen force. They wouldn't move no matter how hard I tried. And yet when I woke they moved quite easily. Though perhaps a bit slowly. And they tingled as though they had slept too.

I always found it funny that your limbs can fall asleep. Mother used to describe it as tiny needles poking into her foot. That seemed more painful than it felt to me. I just thought it kind of tickled a little bit. But Mother must have been tickled too, because she would always laugh when it happened to her. I missed her. And I suddenly remembered the important thing I needed to do. I needed to go home.

I knew the sun wasn't awake yet, and there was still the trickle of rain outside the cottage. Myra and Hudson were still there, and Uncle was truly sound asleep. I knew now was the time to take my leave. I knew it, but I couldn't bring myself to do it. And yet it was now or never. So, it had to be now.

***

I gently tiptoed out from under Uncle Cheech's arm so as not to wake him. I grabbed my small suitcase I brought with me the first night I arrived and slowly opened the front door to step out onto the porch. It was just first light and still sprinkling outside. I knew it was going to seem unfamiliar. And there was a good chance I could get lost. Or even killed. But I kind of figured that was being a little overly dramatic. So, I mustered some grit and stepped off the safety of the porch. Down into the front yard, beneath the tree I knew so well. I walked on to the path that lead to the wall where I first met August. And I continued to follow the path. Right up to the wall and even beyond it. I knew the first hills and even recognized one that shouldn't have been there. But I had seen it somewhere else in Cyrandor. So, I climbed it and continued down the other side to a new path. I saw trees that looked familiar, and some that were not.

And all the while, I kept on. Not knowing if I was headed home, or deeper into a Cyrandor I never knew. While the sun continued to rise, I saw very little of it through the rain. I didn't know if I would meet August or Jasper or Titus, or Mr. Dixon, or Mr. Blake or anyone else on my way. I didn't know too many people in Cyrandor who would have ventured out in the rain. But I did. Maybe I was the first to do it. Maybe I was the only one foolish enough to do it. But maybe I was the only one wise enough to make the choice to do it. To make my own choice. To decide for myself that I could make it in Cyrandor. Or that I could make it on my own.

And I HAD made it on my own. I had been alone in Cyrandor. In the rain. For hours already. And I was okay. If not a little lonely. And it wasn't the first time.

***

I should have thought to bring a snack, because I was starting to get a little hungry. Not so hungry that I was ready to spear a fish or anything. But I was hungry all the same. And it was the first moment I thought of turning back. Because at Uncle's cottage was my cousin. And the Heckella Root. And it could make anything taste savory. I did have the one little bottle I collected for myself, but the Heckella Root on its own couldn't be very filling.

I pulled up one of the tall grasses on the path that resembled the onion grass from back home. And I began to chew on it a bit as I walked on. The flavor wasn't quite as strong as I remembered, but it held me over for a bit. I scooped up a small branch too that I could use as a walking stick. I hoped it would pull me along a bit as my legs began to tire. I thought of taking a break somewhere, but apart from sitting down in the middle of a soggy field, there didn't seem to be a place to rest.

I looked around for a tree or a rock to sit on, but it was just open field as far as I could see. Which didn't happen to be very far at that moment because the rain began to pick up quite a bit. And when I say quite a bit, I mean that it began to come down heavily. So, I started to run. I didn't know where to run, but I ran. I ran down the hillside onto the new path at its base. I ran toward the rainbow that crossed over the stream. I ran along the bank and across a log to the other side. I ran up the new hill and into a forest of tall white leafless trees. And though the leaves were gone, the trees seemed to shield me from the rain. So much so that the ground beneath them was completely dry. As though rain had never touched it. And yet it seemed to be perfectly healthy ground without the rain. So, I decided to rest there. For a moment. Just to catch my breath. And to give my legs a break. I decided to rest. And I did.

***

"Rosa," I heard August whisper. "Where are you going?"

And I jolted awake. "August," I whispered into the forest. I hoped he was really there, but I knew I had only just dreamed it. I whispered his name again, "August!"

And the third time was not a whisper. In fact, I shouted it loud enough that I could hear the tops of the trees clatter together in the wake of my voice. But still August didn't respond. I wondered if I should have left without him. Or at least without telling him. Or Uncle Cheech. Surely Uncle would worry. Wouldn't he? Wouldn't Myra and Hudson worry?

I pulled out Father's timepiece for a moment. And I held them, my mother and father, in the palm of my hand. "Dear God, I miss them. And I miss Uncle and Myra. Would you tell them I'm okay?" God didn't answer me. Not out loud. But I knew He was listening to me. And I knew that somehow, He would get them the message.

CHAPTER TWENTY-TWO

I liked the tall trees. I liked being dry. And I continued under their canopy for a long while. Nearly until dark. Or what seemed like "dark" anyway. It was hard to tell, the further into the forest I got. I couldn't see much of the green landscape I had come to know as Cyrandor. There were still rainbows. Even in the shadows of the trees. And it remained rainless beneath them. But the further away from the open field I got, the less I noticed the daylight. And the more I began to get frightened.

Darkness can do that to you. Mother always left a lamp on to avoid the darkness. I'm not sure if it was for my sake or hers. Mothers are often very brave. But I know that mothers can be afraid sometimes too. And in the dark, so can anyone. So, I thought, perhaps, I ought to find the edge of the forest once again. Just for the light. Or for what remained of the light. But I knew I was very far away from the edge. And for the first time on my journey, I felt very foolish. Not for being afraid, but for being so far away from something safe.

I began to wonder about my particular forest. I wondered if being dry was worth being afraid. But the more I thought about being afraid, the more afraid I got. So, I had to not. I instead held onto my timepiece. And I held onto Mother and Father. And I continued to walk toward the edge of the forest. Or to where I thought the edge of the forest ought to be.

But Cyrandor is a funny place. And the more I walked the darker it still got. And the trees began to let a drop or two of rain past their branches. Perhaps only a drop or two. But all the same, it wasn't quite as dry as it had been before.

***

If it were only for the darkness I could have been fine. But the darker it got, the more noises I heard. Sometimes the wind could whistle. Sometimes the branches could creak. And sometimes.

Sometimes.

Well.

There was another sound that was the most unsettling. It had pieces of laughter in it. And the voices of chipmunks. Or some small creature. But the sound itself was not from a small creature. And I couldn't be sure what it was exactly. But when I heard it, my feet stopped. My whole self stopped. Even the movement of the trees stopped. I was frozen with fear until I could once again convince myself to take another step.

Each time the sound would subside for a while, and I could continue my search for the edge of the forest. But each time it sounded again it brought with it a little more rain. These were the secrets of Cyrandor I had never learned of. Perhaps they were the secrets no one had.

Perhaps it's silly, but the deeper I got, the more inward I became. It started with my shoulders. I began to bring them up toward my ears and inward in an effort to hide my neck. My head even lowered into them. I hunched over a bit and eventually got down on my knees to crawl. If I had wanted to stop moving I would have curled into a ball and hoped the forest around me would disappear. But I feared stopping. So, I kept moving forward. On my knees at times and on my feet when I felt bolder. Never did I stop until the forest became so dark that I couldn't see.

**

I slowed near a large white trunk, its color the only sort of light available. I wrapped my arms around it as far as I could, but it was thicker than my arms could reach. And feeling the safety of something to hold onto, I slowly lowered my body to sit beneath it. I grasped the large roots streaming out on either side of me and leaned against its base. I prayed over and over again. And I tucked my knees up into my chest. And I prayed again. And then once more. I feared every moment that night. Whether I was awake or asleep, I was afraid. And I was praying. And I was worrying. I was hearing every occurrence of that awful sound and feeling every solitary drop of rain. I was cold. And damp. And scared. And holding on to that very large tree as if my life depended on it. Because it did. For whatever was making that sound could either eat me, or leave me be. And I prayed it was the latter.

And it must have been. Because after many sleeps and many wakes, I began to see images around me again. So, either the darkness had weakened, or my eyes had sharpened. But I was still me. I was not the dinner of what I imagined were something of a ferocious teddy bear with fur like the wool of a sheep. Why I imagined it that way, I'm not sure. Perhaps I dreamed of it. But I never saw the creature. And heard even less of it in my newly wakened state.

And because I could begin to see, I braved again the once-sheltering, now-frightening forest for the clearing I longed for so deeply. And perhaps August would be waiting there for me. Waiting to take me home or back to Uncle Cheech. Either place would be a welcome journey.

But though the forest got lighter as I walked, there was still no clearing. No edge to speak of. The forest just grew bigger and wider, it seemed. I began to wonder if I would ever venture out of it. And even if I found a way out of the forest, where would I end up? Would I be in Cyrandor still? Will I have found a way home? Will I have managed to find some other enchanted city?

Am I really fit to make my own decisions? I have made some terrible ones for sure. And they were small decisions. And if I can't be trusted with the small ones, maybe I SHOULD have someone else decide the big ones. Like who I should marry. Or IF I should marry. And just as I began to lose hope in my journey; as quickly as I began to doubt myself; as swiftly as the light returned to the forest and the rain disappeared, it disappeared beyond the forest as well. And I caught a peek beyond the forest.

Before me was a large sea which reflected the unobstructed sunlight in its waters. The waves were small, but they crested in the open waters as well as on the shore. There was no land on the other side. Not that I could find. It was just the sea. No boats. No islands. No swimmers. Just the sea.

And a peculiar bridge that stretched out over it, but ended suspended above it. As though it was one half of a draw bridge left wide open, with nothing on the other side to return to.

***

I stood at the edge of the bridge and looked out over the waters. Still I could see nothing on the other side. Nothing but a crisp horizon where I assumed the sun had come from. I looked below me into the water and saw my reflection. Not a crisp one, but I saw it. If even for a moment. And a rainbow almost beneath the water. It was not very deep, the sea. At least, at the shore. And so I returned from the bridge and walked down by the water's edge.

A few steps into the water and the sand shifted ever so slightly. I feared it would swallow me up, so I quickly stepped back. I looked quickly for a good skipping rock and found a few some yards away. The first I threw right into the sand, hoping to see whether it would be gobbled up by the sea's floor. But it wasn't. Sand, you know, just moves with the waves.

So again, I took some steps into the water and learned the feel of the sand. I pulled another skipping stone from my pocket and gave it a toss. It didn't skip as well in the waves as it would have in the creek. I pulled out another and held it carefully the way Jasper had taught me and gave it another flick of the wrist. It skipped a couple of times, but not for long. Again, it settled into the sea.

One last time and it sailed beautifully over the waves, skipping six times before dropping. I threw my hands up in victory the way Jasper had done. And I smiled to myself. Jasper would have been proud of me. I suddenly felt very lonely again. And I walked back up the bridge to the edge.

It was a strong, sturdy bridge. It didn't show wear from too many uses. It didn't look bruised or broken. It just seemed to be only half of a bridge. You could see the water between the large wooden planks. And I was fascinated by how it moved beneath me as I hovered over it. I gazed once again across to the horizon and wished I could see sailboats or large ships moving gracefully across the water. And I didn't.

***

But just off to the right, at the very edge of the horizon, was something I hadn't noticed before. It was land. And it seemed to be growing and making its way across the horizon like a ship on the move. Still a very small thin line, but one that was growing. And on the move.

CHAPTER TWENTY-THREE

With break of day my hunger hadn't waned, and I wondered when my next meal might come. And on top of that, the air had started to grow colder the more I walked along the sea's edge. It was a long journey beside it, and often I sat to rest. My increasing hunger made it ever more difficult. Occasionally, I drank from the sea to improve my strength, but I found nothing to eat along the way. More than once I considered returning to the forest in effort to find a fruit or sap from the trees. But I feared the forest. And not so much the trees themselves but that one unusual sound from within. That one unfamiliar creature who made me the focus of his next meal. And, more than anything, I wanted to eat. But not to be eaten.

I pulled out my jacket and prepared for my return to the forest. I had a plan. If the darkness grew too thick I would stay as close to the edge and near the coast as possible. If I couldn't find my way out I was prepared to fight. If I could handle Jasper, I could handle the laughing chipmunk. It really didn't sound so scary when you think of it that way. But still it was. Even through every ounce of determination I could muster.

I stepped into the forest.

∗∗∗

It wasn't so bad. I remembered what I liked about it the first time. The pretty white trees. The sounds they made as they clacked together in the wind. The safety and comfort of their solid round bases. It was strengthening. I felt bolder. Stronger. Wiser. And I journeyed on. Until it began to get dark.

I started to veer once again toward the edge. Just to be safe. But I couldn't recall which direction the edge had been. I had been in the forest for hours again. Gleaning courage. And searching for food. I had turned myself around. Forgetting entirely where I had come from. Once again, I found myself lost. And all that strength and confidence began to weaken. The fear crept back in, and I knew the utter darkness was too close-by.

I paused for a moment. I grazed the base of a tree with my fingertips. It was smooth. And warm. So different from the evening air. I shivered. Because of the cold, but also for what lay before me. Why hadn't Uncle come after me? I'd give anything to be found and rescued by him now. Even if it meant having to get married. In truth, I had envisioned the not-so-terrible suitors I could be betrothed to. And I'd really even give anything to be rescued by one of them by now. Namely, Jasper.

But he wasn't coming. And neither was Uncle. And so, I had to keep going.

***

It didn't take long. It came pretty much with the darkness. The laughter. The squeak. The collision of the trees. And a warm moist feeling approaching my wrist. I looked down but couldn't see anything in the night. It came in measured rhythms like it was keeping time. Or panting. Something was breathing. And so near to me that I could feel its breath on my wrist. I clenched my fist for protection. If it bit there would be more meat for it to get through before crushing my bones.

But it didn't bite. Instead I felt the dull claws of two small hands wrapping around my knee. It seemed to be preparing to climb. More of my muscles tensed. I prayed as I began to plan my escape. But escape didn't seem to be my body's plan. It wouldn't budge. Not one muscle. While whatever it was continued to climb.

I felt it rolling up over my shoulder and the warm breath was now concentrated on my neck. It's laughter sounds were louder and more terrible next to my ear. I could feel it start with my hair.

At last my muscles released and I dropped to my knees, grabbing hold of the wiry-furred creature that resembled nothing of a teddy bear. It anchored its dull claws into my shoulder and back as it hissed when I took hold. I tried to pull it off but found it dug in deeper to resist. It hurt. And I went all the way down hoping to knock the creature off with a blow to the ground.

It held on tight and I felt a painful tug at my scalp as I was sure it ripped a small lock of hair from my head. I cringed and let out a shout of pain. In that brief moment of voice, it seemed to cause the white tree trunks to glow for a moment. And in their glow, I spied the shadow of a horse. It reared up, kicking its front legs majestically in the darkness.

Again, I shouted out, and again the trees pulsed with light. And I heard a whisper before the creature stole away. What remained was just the horse. Or rather, August. And myself. And the empty white forest. And the occasional clatter of the trees.

***

It was peaceful. And safe. I knew August was disappointed in me, but he didn't say so. I shouldn't have run off on my own. But August rescued me all the same. And he sat with me. In silence, but he sat with me. And we waited for dawn's light.

My jacket was ripped from the struggle and my shoulder bled ever so slightly. It hurt, but it was a minor wound. I knew I'd recover. I just wished there was something for the pain. And there was. August was there. And that was enough. I was going to be okay.

"August," I started. He bobbed his head as if to urge me to go on. "I'm betrothed." But August knew that. He probably knew that's why I left.

"Rosa," he answered back. "You know I have to leave you."

But I didn't. Not now. I surely couldn't have learned everything. Not enough for him to go. And my sense of safety began to fade once again.

"You can't leave me, August!" I cried. "You can't!"

But he wasn't going to leave me in the forest. But I was learning enough that it would soon be time. He told me he would help me get home. But he meant, of course, back to Uncle's. And then, very soon, I wouldn't see him anymore. Except for when I was in "truly great need."

"But truly great need," he said, "is incredibly rare." And I knew that it was. But all the same, I was at peace knowing he was with me now. And I was going to be okay.

CHAPTER TWENTY-FOUR

As we neared the end of the forest I could see that it had begun to snow. They were very light flakes and I looked forward to seeing Cyrandor in the snow. It was always a pretty scene. And I suspected even more so in Cyrandor. We had walked most of the daylight. Sometimes I rode. And sometimes I walked beside him. But August was kind and he made sure I made it safely to the forest edge.

Dusk had settled in by the time I caught sight of the clearing. And across the small snowy lane was a large, stately building. It was a couple stories high and stretched wide from end to end. On the porch were four towering white pillars. And the sign post in front read in curly letters, "Cyrandor Inn."

August strode right up to the front stairs and I leapt down. "I'll be just over here," he said as he urged me to step inside. "You need food and warmth. I'll be alright." I watched him step over to the side of the building before I went up the steps and opened the door. The windows in the front were in tiny square sections. Some were frosted. Some collected a small amount of snow. And still one other had a tiny crack that ran from corner to corner.

***

Inside were the beginnings of Christmas garland being hung on banisters and doorways. There was a long wooden counter with a wall of mailboxes and keys behind it. Three aproned ladies bustled about sorting mail, sweeping the floor and reviewing the guestbook.

One had short curly hair and saw me approach. She looked up through a wide grin and a few missing teeth. Nevertheless, her smile was warm. "Rosa!" she exclaimed with inexplicable joy. I smiled at the reception.

"Yes," I nodded. "My name is Rosa and I—"

"Of course, you are, Dear," added the second. She was delightfully plump and wore bright red lipstick. "We've your room all fixed up for you. Would you like a cup of tea?"

Before I could answer the third woman put down the stack of mail and "Oh dear! I think a roast would be in better order. Look at her, the poor thing!"

"Oh, I do think you're right," the first one added. "Step right into the kitchen, Love. We'll fix you right up."

And before I could accept I was nearly pushed through the doorway into a wooden chair next to a long wooden table. It was already set with shakers of salt and pepper. And another familiar seasoning.

***

I glanced over at the older couple a few tables over. They had finished their dinner already and were sipping from teacups which they perfectly placed back into their saucers. Occasionally they would glance my way and whisper. When they did I would look back down. I was the young stranger who ran away from home. I was sure they had heard of me too.

The bright lipsticked lady from the entry returned in a hurry from the kitchen and shuffled over next to me, pulling out a chair to join me. "We've some rolls coming soon and then a nice hearty meal. We'll get you fixed up in no time." And she sat down.

I wasn't sure quite how to respond so, "Thank you," is what came after a silent moment. Then she continued.

"Oh, don't think of it!" she exclaimed. And then, "We've sent word to the Guardian of your arrival and he'll receive you in the morning." I knew Uncle must be very upset. I knew that what I had done was awful. But they've called the Guardian on me. I knew *of* the Guardian but have never met him. He's something of a mayor, they told me. Well, Mr. Dixon told me. Way back when we first met. Only Mr. Dixon had never met him either. So, he must stay away from the residents of Cyrandor, unless you've done something really bad. Like run away. In the rain.

I gripped my glass of water and took a gulp. I had taken the salt shaker to shift in my hands to keep busy. Lipstick continued to smile at me. I smiled back to be friendly. She was being very nice to me. Even with all the trouble I was in. "Is the Guardian…" I began, wondering how to go on.

"What is it, Rosa?" she asked.

"Is he…well…am I in trouble, ma'am?"

***

And then the rolls came out. They were slathered in butter. Six of them. Each one so hot that when I plucked one out of the basket to eat I felt my fingertips burn. But I pretended they didn't. And I dug my teeth right into it, hoping that Lipstick would forget what I had just asked. But she didn't.

"Oh gracious, no, Miss Rosa! He's been wantin' to see ya for a good long piece, now."

"Me?" I asked bewildered and through a mouthful of freshly baked dough. "What for?"

"Oh, I suppose everyone's eager ta know ya, my dear. Even meself, you see." She paused for a moment and probably wondered at the bewilderment on my face. "Oh, I beg yer pardon, Miss. My name's Evelyn. Evelyn Toscer." That was a much prettier name than Lipstick, which up til now was all I could think to call her. So, I was glad she introduced herself. And I stuck out my hand to shake hers. When I did, she pulled a towel from her shoulder and wiped the butter off my hand before taking it. It was friendly though. Not in a scolding way.

"I appreciate your kind hospitality, Mrs. Toscer," I said after I had swallowed. "Why does everyone want to meet me?" I thought for once in Cyrandor I was about to get a straight answer. Right to the point. No putting me off or changing the subject. I had asked. And Evelyn would answer. She was that kind of lady.

"Per…haps I should let the Guardian speak to you about that. I'll be gettin' yer roast now." And she was gone. Back through the door to the kitchen. Back out with a plate full of roast beef and green beans and mashed potatoes and corn. And as soon as the plate hit the table, she was off again to the entryway. Never answering my question. And not lingering long enough for me to ask again. Cyrandor, at the very least, did not like direct questions.

***

I polished it off. The whole plate. Even the green beans. I don't ordinarily like them. But when you're as hungry as I was (and you have a shaker of Heckella Root available), they're not so bad. So, I ate them. Then the first lady with the curly hair showed me to my room. It was up the stairs and down the hall to the right. Number 22. On the end. She even left me with the key. I had never had a key to my own room before. I sat down on the bed and peered out the window. It was dark again, but the light reflected off the newly blanketed landscape outside.

August stood below, eating snow and shuffling his feet. He was a very pretty horse and I truly had missed him. I was glad he had come to rescue me, even if I wasn't sure I was ready to go back yet. Curly reappeared with an extra blanket as it was "startin' to get mighty cold outside, now. Perhaps you'll want this. And if you need anything else, dear, you just ring old Fitz, now ya hear?"

"Old Fitz?" I asked.

"Evelyn Fitz. That's me, Miss Rosa." I smirked. Two Evelyns. In one inn. That seemed just like Cyrandor somehow. "Ya know, there's three of us," she went on. "Of course, you already met Ev' Toscer. And the other is Mrs. Rothbottom. We're a funny lot, the three of us." And I knew they must be. And I thanked her again for giving me a place to stay the night.

***

I was much happier to be in the Inn than out in the forest. But still I laid awake a long time before finally dozing off. When I did, I dreamt of the creature in the forest. And of Grandpa and Uncle Cheech. And Myra and William. And Jasper. I realized how much I missed them all. And I was eager to get back to them at last. But I was afraid of the Guardian. I wasn't sure I wanted morning to come. Because I didn't know this Guardian. And I was afraid of what kind of impression he would have of me.

I woke much earlier than I usually do. But I couldn't seem to fall back to sleep. I just laid there thinking of my dreams. And of what was to come. And wishing so badly I could hug my mother and father and know that whatever it was would be alright.

I peered again out the window at the morning. There stood August. Some newly fallen snow had collected on his mane. And a small tree appeared nearby that I didn't notice last night in the darkness. It was a familiar one. With a familiar treat. And I looked forward to helping myself to one before I left the Inn. But August was ahead of me. He sunk his teeth into a candy apple on a lower branch. It was apparently a bit of trouble as it appeared to stick to him and he tossed and pranced a bit to knock it loose before it dropped to the ground. As it hit, it split apart, and he continued to consume the candied treat. I chuckled at the episode before deciding to get dressed and return to the two Evelyns and Mrs. Rothbottom downstairs.

***

There was a knock at the door. A stately knock. And I opened it timidly. A tall, slender man in a bowtie held out a silver tray with a small card on it. I reached up to retrieve it. As I began to open it, he interrupted with a bit of a chuckle in his voice. "You won't be able to read it, Miss. The Guardian has terrible handwriting. He'd like you to join him in the dining room for some breakfast if you're willing."

"Oh, of course," I said as I reached for my things. But he stopped me.

"I'll need to relay the message first, Miss. The Guardian must first hear that you've *accepted* his invitation before you *arrive* at his invitation." So, I paused. And he was silent and still. Finally, "Would you write it down, Miss?" I looked at him puzzled. "He pretends to read, though he can't. And then he blames his eyesight and demands I read it to him. It needn't be fancy. I can embellish." I smirked. I kind of liked the man in the bowtie. He was funny. So, I took the card and scribbled a verse from my book report and handed it back. "Thank you, Miss. I shall return in a moment." And he left.

I sat back down and peered out the window again. It seemed August had helped himself to another apple. He nodded at a gentleman ascending the steps of the Inn. The man nodded back. I thought it peculiar until I recognized the man as my Uncle Cheech. Immediately my heart began to pound. What would he say to me? How would I explain? Or did he even know I was here? But he must have, because he exchanged nods with August. And so, August must have been the one to tell him. But August has been there the entire time. Hasn't he? Or did he leave in the night? Why don't I know these things? After all, I am still a spy, aren't I? I know I'm still learning, but shouldn't these be things I can keep track of?

***

I considered ignoring the Guardian's invitation. I thought of staying tucked away in my room. Or sneaking down the back stairway – if they have a back stairway. But I knew I had to face him. I knew I couldn't continue to run away. So, I opened the door and stepped out into the hallway. I slowly made my way toward the entryway and down the stairs. There behind the desk was Mrs. Rothbottom. She greeted me warmly before I heard a gentleman's voice coming through the doorway, "Good morning, Evelyn." But it wasn't my Uncle. And I looked around for one of the Evelyns. They were nowhere to be seen.

"Good morning, Your Honor," responded Mrs. Rothbottom.

"I understand you've the young Rosa staying here, is that right?" She nodded my direction. "Oh, thank you," he nodded.

I remained motionless on the third step. He walked my direction. I continued to glance past him occasionally, wondering where my Uncle had gone. "Rosa, it's nice to meet you," he said as he stuck out his hand. I took it. "I'm what people call the Guardian. I was supposed to meet you here this morning and give you the rundown, see, of all things Cyrandor. But I just got your message and it appears you know all about it." I continued to stare at him.

"My message, sir? I mean, Your Honor?" I responded at last.

"Oh, just call me Sol. That Guardian business, that's just a title. We're equals you and me."

"Equals? You mean—" I stopped again. Now is my chance. The Guardi—I mean Sol was supposed to give me the "rundown of all things Cyrandor." Now is my chance to finally learn it all. "Well, Sol, sir, I—" I began.

"Just Sol, Rosa. You don't need to add the sir. Let's go in here and see Cheech." My uncle! He was here! So, I followed Sol into the dining room. And there he sat. He had removed his hat and hung it on the back of his chair. He looked up when I entered, and a smile spread across his face. And I knew at that very moment he wasn't mad at me anymore. If he ever was to begin with.

CHAPTER TWENTY-FIVE

Uncle stood right up, came over to me and hugged me as hard as he could. And just as he was about to let go, he swatted me right on my seat and told me, "Don't you ever do that to us again." It hurt a little. But only for a moment.

"Yes, sir," I said. And then he giggled and pulled out my chair for me.

"Well, Cheech," said Sol, "it seems my work here is done. Sounds like your niece knows all she needs to know." And he reached to shake Uncle's hand. My jaw dropped.

"Thanks for finding her," said Uncle as they shook. And he added a pat on the Guardian's shoulder. As Sol slipped out of the dining room and out the door of the Inn, down the steps, I turned back to Uncle unable to speak. In my head, I was shouting at him.

"Why did you send him away?" I wanted to ask. I didn't know anything about what I'm supposed to know. And how did he get that idea anyway? I needed to know why I was—

"Relax, Rosa. We're going to talk about it right now," he said, interrupting my mental berating. And almost as if on cue, the Evelyns and Mrs. Rothbottom came bustling in to offer us eggs and potatoes and waffles and sausages. I enjoyed them, but I wished they would go away so Uncle could tell me what he needed to tell me – what I needed to know. "Thank you very much, but can you give my niece and me a moment," Uncle said kindly.

"Oh, of course," responded Toscer as she hurried into the kitchen.

"Evelyn, could you check back in on them in a moment?" asked Old Fitz to Mrs. Rothbottom.

Evelyn? I wondered again. All three of them are Evelyn?

"Yes, all three," whispered my Uncle.

"For certain, I will," responded Mrs. Rothbottom. But I hadn't asked it out loud. And I realized at that moment that Uncle's spy capabilities were highly refined. He could hear my thoughts.

***

"I could read your face," said my Uncle. "They're a sweet covey of quail for sure." He meant the Evelyns, but I had never heard that expression attributed in that fashion. And then he went on. "Rosa, you and I are family. And we have a special job as a family. First and foremost, we look out for each other. That's what this all boils down to. You're here in Cyrandor because your mother and father are looking out for you. You're staying with me because I'm looking out for you. Myra and William, they come to visit so they can look out for you. Your Grandpa, he's looking out for you too. And you're betrothed because we all want the best for you. But betrothals are similar to proposals. It's just an offer put forth by the parents. It is up to you to accept or decline. And he can do the same."

"So, that's why I'm here." I stated calmly.

"Well, yes, in part. But there's more. You see—" I stopped him. My mind drifted to the image of August outside my window. He was a beautiful horse. And a precious friend.

"Please, don't go on. Not yet." Uncle was surprised but nodded his okay.

"Can I at least introduce you to the young man you may someday find it in your heart to marry?" I hesitated. If my betrothal wasn't all I needed to know and that there was more, then maybe it was okay to find out who he was. I waited. And then smiled to myself as a thought struck me.

"Okay," I answered. And I was right. Uncle motioned to a table near the wall behind me, where sat my cousin Myra, her husband William, and a messy-haired boy named Jasper. Jasper was even in his church clothes as though this was something important. I rolled my eyes and pretended to gag as he walked over. But inside I was happy. For now.

"Hi-ya Rosa," Jasper said, with a little less energy than usual.

"Hi, Jasper," I responded. It was awkward. But the moment passed quickly and soon we were just eating breakfast and talking about normal stuff, not marriage and betrothals. I felt better knowing that I could choose *not* to marry him. But I felt a little scared that instead he would choose not to marry me.

***

Uncle said I could walk home with August and that he would take Myra and William and Jasper home. I was a little afraid to be alone again. But I wanted to be, all the same. And I knew August would take care of me. The Evelyns sent me with an extra blanket in case of the snow or a "colder cold." And Uncle kissed me goodbye before we left. Atop my head, of course. And I'd see him back at the cottage in an hour or so.

But I thought about asking August to take me back to the shore. Near the bridge.

"Not just now," he said. "I think you need to be getting home. Perhaps another day." But I knew that other day would be a long way away. Or not at all.

We walked mostly along the forest, down the snowy path. It was a sunny day. And Cyrandor's beauty was more real than ever. I put my hands in my jacket pocket as we walked along and discovered a small card in my left one. Pulling it out, I noticed it was an invitation. To the "Guardian's Ball." And it was addressed to me. And a guest.

"He must have thought well of you, Rosa. That invitation is hard to come by," assured August. I smiled and stuck it back in my pocket. And I sat a little taller. And wondered who to bring with me.

When we began to turn away from the forest a figure in the distance was running toward us. As he got closer I could see it was Jasper and he was alone. I hopped down from August and we stopped a moment.

"Jasper," I called. "What is it?"

"It's your Uncle," he said, slightly out of breath. "He needs your help. Come quick!" We both climbed back on August and he ran as fast as we had ever gone. Jasper held tightly to his neck and I held tightly to Jasper as we rode.

We slowed down near the wall and meadow where I first met August. There were Myra and William. Myra sat on the wall, William stood beside it. But Uncle Cheech wasn't there. And for a moment, my heart sank in despair.

"He lost consciousness for a moment and took a fall. But he's alright. Mr. Dixon helped him over to Doctor's house. William is going to look in on him in a moment." Myra paused and looked straight at me.

"Will he be okay?" I asked with some desperation. And Myra didn't know, but she pretended he would.

"Jasper and August and I are going to take you home." I could see the three of them exchange glances, and then Jasper whispered something to Myra. "I think that's a very good idea, in fact," she said. And they smiled.

I didn't understand. How could they be so happy all the sudden? But I went with them. Only instead of going back to the cottage we went past it and through the wooded area behind it. I had never gone that way. And I was afraid of what that forest might bring. But it wasn't very long, and soon we were on the other side of it. And once again near the shore. There was a small wooden dock, and one of those long wooden poles that Uncle showed me in his tool shed.

Jasper grabbed my hand and pulled me right out on the dock. Then he pulled a gold chain necklace from his pocket that held a small box. He handed it to me.

I looked at him quizzically and began to open the box.

"Wait!" he shouted. "Don't open it! Inside is the very last secret of Cyrandor. As long as it remains inside the box, you can still see August." I smiled.

"Really?" I asked with hopeful glee.

And Myra sat me down. Jasper too. The three of us on the dock. While August stood nearby.

"Rosa," she began.

CHAPTER TWENTY-SIX

Uncle Cheech lived in this town called Cyrandor. It sounded like some kind of mythical city, with hidden secrets and fantastical adventures. Cyrandor. For eight months.

Grandpa never said why.

But Myra did.

***

We went that evening to look in on Uncle Cheech. He was awake and smiling, but I could tell he was tired. Doctor said he just needs his rest and he'll be back on his feet in no time. He urged William and Myra to stay in Cyrandor with me a few days more, until Uncle was better. And they thought it would be right. Because as Uncle says, we are family. And our first job is to look out for each other. And Myra said so too. At Doctor's, but also on the dock that afternoon.

You see, in Cyrandor, my family is royalty. And we have a special job. Myra didn't say we were spies, but I knew we were. What Myra said is that first and foremost we look out for each other. But second is that we look out for Cyrandor. It *is* a mythical type of city with hidden secrets and fantastical adventures. And it takes eight months to discover them. And to accept them.

Myra and Jasper and I walked along the coast for a moment. And as we walked we came to a bridge. It looked an awful lot like the bridge I saw before. It extended out over the water and remained suspended there with no other end. Like one half of a draw bridge lowered and awaiting its mate.

And as we looked across the water, near the horizon was a small tract of land with an equal and opposite bridge. Or so it appeared in the distance.

Cyrandor floats away when it rains, Myra told me. It floats right down the ocean until the rain stops. And when the rain stops, it has to return to its natural spot. And that's where we come in. We are the Gondoliers, or "Groundskeepers." That's who Uncle is. And who my Mother would have been, until she married my father. And who Myra would have been until she married William. So now it is up to me. If I accept my betrothal, then I accept my position in the family. And I shall become what my Uncle was when he retires.

I looked at Jasper, but only for a moment. It seemed he was afraid I would refuse. But it wasn't only my decision. And as he glanced back at me, I looked away again. Somewhat frightened that even he would refuse. Or worse. That he wouldn't.

I don't have to decide right away. I can wait until I'm grown (which in Cyrandor is 18 years old). But I can visit any time I want (or at least when the rain causes Cyrandor to catch up with home). But once I accept my position, then I must stay.

So that book I wrote about, it was about us. It was about Calvin, my Uncle Cheech. And Uncle was growing tired. So even though I had until my 18th birthday to decide. Part of me knew it was a decision that might come earlier. Even now. And before I could ask, Myra took my hand and prayed for her father. For my Uncle Cheech. There was no question whether I would do the job in his absence. We were family. But betrothal or no, I prayed that Uncle could continue for a long time to come. Even past my 18th birthday.

***

I fingered the invitation in my pocket and looked from Jasper to Myra, as they continued. I wondered if they had received a similar invitation. We walked back to the dock and then to the cottage. Myra sent Jasper back home as we met William and went to see Uncle.

I sat on the edge of the bed and leaned into Uncle's side as we all huddled together in conversation. I again fingered the invitation in my pocket and pulled it out to look at it.

"What have you got there?" Uncle asked.

"It says I can bring a guest," I answered. And I handed him the card. "Would you like to go, Uncle Cheech?" I asked. And he would. And we did. Because Doctor said it would be okay, as long as I let him rest between dances.

So, while we rested, Uncle and I, I decided to ask one more question. "Where did you go, when Grandpa stayed with me?" And he finally answered me. He had gone to see Mother and Father. Not in a graveyard. But at home. At my home. For he knew the time was coming for me to learn of my station. And he promised them that he would see them, and they would know, before he told me. And he did. And they did.

And they were well and happy, and they missed me ever so much. Uncle said it was more than I missed them, but I doubted it. But the rule is that they couldn't interfere with my eight months, so I just never knew.

Cyrandor for eight months. Almost. As far as Jasper was concerned there was just one more task to complete.

***

Myra wrapped a blanket around my head as it hung down like a veil and picked the prettiest flowers. Jasper grabbed my hand and walked me to the end of the dock. I with my blanket veil and my flowers in my hand. He with the gold chain with the box containing Cyrandor's final secret.

At the end of the dock stood August. Myra had made a floral wreath for his head, too. Jasper placed the chain over my head and around my neck.

"And by the power vested in me," said August, "which is really no power at all as far as this is concerned, I now pronounce you husband and wife," he paused, "to be."

And Jasper kissed my cheek.

And I wiped it off with my blanket veil.

EPILOGUE

They say you're to live happily ever after. And we probably would. But we didn't need to yet. And Jasper knew that we weren't really married.

So, August and I stood near the porch of Uncle's cottage. Myra and William had gone back home. So had Jasper. And Uncle was inside resting. This was my final week in Cyrandor.

August told me that I didn't have to decide yet. And that the choice was still and always mine. Then he told me that I'd have to try. Just once. For Uncle. For myself. And for Cyrandor. I wasn't sure what he meant until he took me back to the dock. He kicked at the long pole, so I picked it up. It was heavy. But not as heavy as I expected.

I put one end into the water and he shook his head. "Not just yet, Rosa. Up there." And he nodded to the treetops.

"You want me to climb the trees?" I asked.

"Not the trees," and he nodded again. I noticed the thin swirl of smoke coming from Uncle's chimney. "There," he said. And we trekked back through the trees to the cottage – to the backside of the cottage. A small wooden ladder leaned unassumingly against the house. "There," August said again.

I gave him a quizzical glance and started up. When I first looked, it didn't go very high. But as I kept climbing there was always another rung to reach. Until I could step out on the roof. It peaked in the middle the way roofs do. So, I sat down with a leg on either side, and the pole to my right.

Mr. Dixon's poem came to mind and I uttered the words quietly. "Take thee, Wind, and lead us straight. Mind thee, Rain, our blessed fate. If fate be found, then quick thy gait. And be not lost nor be not late,"

As I started to cast it downward, it touched land. Not next to the cottage, but behind and at the bottom of the sea.

"Now push, Rosa!" called a voice from below. "And Cyrandor can once again journey back home," it said again with every confidence. But it wasn't August. And it wasn't Uncle. Nor Myra, nor William, nor Grandpa, nor Jasper. It was my Father. And next to him was my Mother, smiling proudly.

So, I did. And so, it went.

THE END

www.ingramcontent.com/pod-product-compliance
Lightning Source LLC
Chambersburg PA
CBHW021048130626
46552CB00005B/2072